The Cowlick Crown

Goutham Ekollu

First Edition

ISBN:

Paperback: 979-8-9931471-0-9

Audio Book: 979-8-9931471-1-6

e-book: 979-8-9931471-2-3

Published in the USA

My family, my friends,

and all who taught me to see

The Art of Failure

"Gotcha!" Kaya roared, executing a flawless forty-three-degree pounce onto her target.

She landed face-first in a pit of rotting mangoes.

The stench hit her like a wall. Gagging, she spat out pulp while smaller animals scattered. A family of toucans covered their beaks; even the buzzards looked disgusted.

"Surprise!" Finn leapt from his hiding spot with jazz hands. "Did you see that trajectory? Perfect ten-point landing. Right into my trap."

"You made me fall into garbage!" Kaya sputtered. Pulp dripped from her whiskers.

"It's not garbage, it's set decoration. I was going for 'tropical surprise with hints of decomposition.'"

"I'm going to kill you," Kaya snarled.

"But did you see how gracefully you fell?" Finn grinned. "I've been working on those pit angles for weeks."

From her perch high above, Nugget watched the chaos. The small, fluffy chicken's distinctive cowlick stuck up like a tiny mohawk.

"This is not going according to plan," Kaya howled below.

"Nothing ever goes according to plan," Finn called back. "That's why you need style!"

Nugget sighed. Six months. Six months since this insanity began, and it was only getting more elaborate. Last week, Finn rigged a pulley system involving coconuts and a very confused sloth. The week before, Kaya recruited a squirrel squadron as an early warning system, complete with acorn-based communication codes.

All of this. Over her.

How had a simple chicken become the center of a tiger war? The answer, Nugget knew, lay in one perfectly ordinary morning six months ago.

It started simply enough, in the golden heart of the dense jungle reserve. Two tiger cubs, Kaya and Finn, crouched low in the high grass near the farm's fence. But even at nine months old, they approached everything differently.

Kaya studied the coop for three days straight. She mapped the farmer's schedule, recorded the rooster napping times, even counted the number of bowls (six), and calculated the optimal pouncing angle (thirty-two degrees from the left corner post). Her plan was flawless. Foolproof. Perfectly timed.

Finn spent those same three days practicing elaborate leaps off increasingly higher rocks, determined to make the most spectacular entrance in tiger cub history.

Their eyes sparkled with curiosity and mischief as they watched the farmer's coop buzz with excitement. Tiny, fuzzy chicks wobbled on unsteady legs, peeping softly as they explored the coop.

"Look at them," Kaya whispered, consulting the leaf where she sketched the coop layout. "If we approach from the northwest corner at exactly noon, when the farmer goes inside for lunch, we can—"

"Fluffy appetizers with legs!" Finn interrupted, bouncing on his haunches. "I'm going to do a triple backflip and land right in the middle of them. It'll be epic."

Kaya's ears swiveled back in annoyance. "Finn, this requires strategy. You can't just—"

"I call dibs on that one!" Finn said pointing a paw at a particularly wide-eyed chick sporting a feathery cowlick that stuck up like a mohawk.

Without warning, he launched himself toward the fence in an unnecessary somersault.

"What?! No way!" Kaya scrambled after him, her carefully planned approach forgotten. "I've been planning this for three days. You can't just jump in without—"

"Too late," Finn grinned, freezing mid-leap with his paws spread wide. "I called dibs. Jungle law."

"There's no jungle law about dibs," Kaya growled, her cleaner pounce closing the gap. "And definitely none about ridiculous aerial stunts!"

"You'd have to catch me first," Finn laughed, doing an entirely unnecessary spin before landing in a show-off crouch.

Inside the coop, that small, fluffy chick—whom they would later name Nugget, quite ironically—watched this entire display. Even then, she seemed less like prey and more like an audience member at a particularly chaotic circus. While her siblings panicked, she tilted her head, studying the cubs with something that looked suspiciously like interest.

Everything about the chick was unusual. Her distinctive cowlick was hard to miss. She nudged worms through the wire mesh to sulking squirrels. She cooed softly at nervous sparrow chicks until they stopped trembling. She even clucked gentle advice to the farmer's dog about his sore paw. While the other chicks huddled together, this one... noticed. And she cared.

Later that day, chaos struck. Kaya and Finn's bickering escalated until they crashed straight into the

8

coop's fence. The boards splintered, chicks scattered, and feathers flew. Nugget didn't wait for an invitation.

Through the gap in the fence, she saw the jungle stretching wide and green. At that exact moment, the farmer's voice carried from the porch: "Soup tomorrow!"

Nugget's tiny heart skipped. Stew? Soup? Absolutely not.

She bolted. Past the fence, across the grass, into the waiting wild.

Neither cub caught her that day, but both swore they would. Nugget, for her part, found herself oddly curious about this noisy jungle. It smelled of mango and danger, but also freedom.

That night, she roosted in a low branch, watching the stars peek through the canopy. One blinked brightly above her, just as a mango dropped from a nearby tree. Nugget tilted her head, wondering aloud: "Knew that was going to fall."

And so began the surveillance wars, the sabotage competitions, and Nugget's accidental rise from

9

ordinary coop chicken to the jungle's most unlikely prize.

Over time, the tigers' obsession evolved into round-the-clock surveillance—a perfect showcase of how differently they approached everything.

Kaya dubbed her effort "Operation Clucklock," treating it like a full military campaign as she sat in her banyan-tree lookout, smugly reviewing intelligence reports from her squirrel network.

Subject remains secure. Threat Level: manageable. Probability of Finn-related interference: 93%.

Below, beetle-shell chimes swayed in the breeze. Any movement toward Nugget's perch would ring them instantly. Kaya had accounted for wind patterns, leaf fall, and even overenthusiastic monkeys swinging too close. Her system was flawless.

She sipped from her mango smoothie, savoring the quiet.

A squirrel scout scrambled up, tail twitching in the pre-arranged "all clear" signal. Kaya smiled—perfect.

Then Nugget gave a startled cluck.

Kaya whipped around. There, standing three feet from Nugget and holding out a freshly plucked hibiscus, was Finn. No chimes had rung. No squirrels had sounded the alarm. He looked irritatingly serene.

"Like my entrance?" Finn asked casually. He set the flower down with a bow.

Kaya's eyes narrowed. "How—"

"Oh, you know." He inspected his claws. "Studied your wind patterns for a week. Recruited your third-favorite squirrel—what's his name, Twitchy? —to feed you false tail codes. Even muffled my steps with moss so the chimes wouldn't pick up the vibrations."

"That's... planning." Kaya let the word hang on her tongue, brow furrowed.

Finn grinned. "Sometimes the best style... is strategy."

Before she could respond, he sauntered away, tail high. Kaya stared after him, part furious, part impressed, and completely rethinking her threat assessment.

Nugget, watching from above, tilted her head. They weren't trying to eat her anymore—that much was clear. But what were they trying to prove? And to whom?

Over time, sabotage escalated into an art form.

Kaya convinced a colony of capuchin monkeys to join her "Nugget Protection Task Force," providing them with detailed training manuals carved into bark, scheduled patrol rotations, and a benefits package including three barrels of premium stolen bananas.

Finn retaliated by recruiting overly enthusiastic parrots for "Operation Magnificent Confusion," training them to perform synchronized aerial shows while mimicking Nugget's clucks in perfect harmony, sending Kaya's task force on dozens of wild chicken chases.

"It's performance art meets choreographed confusion," he explained to a very unimpressed tortoise.

One memorable chase ended with Kaya's perfectly planned pursuit route leading directly into Finn's newest creation: a mud pit disguised as a "natural spa experience," complete with floating lily pads and what he insisted were "aromatherapy reeds."

Kaya emerged looking like a swamp monster, her methodical precision in cleaning herself only making the mud distribution more even.

Nugget, witnessing this disaster, screamed and flew directly into the tree above, landing squarely on Finn's face.

"Stop throwing yourself at me," he screeched, blindly flailing as feathers flew everywhere.

"You need better plans!" Kaya howled from below.

"Who needs plans when you have natural talent?" Finn called back, spitting out feathers.

Nugget's frustration peaked. She started holding "Tiger Talks," sitting both tigers down and interrogating them like a feathery therapist with a clipboard made of woven grass.

"Kaya." She adjusted her makeshift beetle-shell spectacles. "Why do you need eighteen backup plans for bringing me a mango?"

"Because plans 1 through 17 account for weather, Finn interference, fruit quality, and optimal timing."

"And Plan 18?"

"Asteroid Impact Contingency."

"Asteroid impact?"

"You never know." Her tone left no room for doubt.

Nugget turned to Finn. "And you—why does delivering a flower require a full costume change and a musical number?"

Finn puffed out his chest. "Because anyone can bring a flower. But only I can bring a flower with *panache*. Did you see my entrance yesterday? I call it 'Tiger in Bloom: A One-Cat Opera.'"

"You fell out of the tree."

"*Dramatically*! It was all part of the artistic vision."

Nugget stared at them both. "You two are exhausting."

She rubbed her beak against her wing, suddenly struck by a thought: *Somewhere along the way, she'd stopped being dinner and started being the scoreboard. Or maybe… the referee.*

The Great Chicken Heist

Three months later, the jungle had accepted an odd fact of life—there was a chicken in residence, and two tiger cubs who wouldn't stop bickering over her.

Nugget had made herself a hammock out of woven leaves and twine scraps, strung between two trees near a clearing. She liked to think of it as "neutral ground," though Kaya called it a *forward operating base* and Finn insisted it was a *stage*.

By now, Nugget's natural curiosity had made her something of a minor celebrity. She couldn't resist poking her beak into other animals' lives. When two monkeys fought over a mango stash, Nugget suggested splitting it down the middle (and claimed the pit for herself, "for research"). She taught a pair of nervous iguanas how to sunbathe in shifts so neither got left out. She even left little scraps of food for the farmer's dog, who sometimes wandered to the jungle's edge with a limp.

It was small, nosy kindnesses like these that made her different. Chickens weren't supposed to care about anyone else's problems. But Nugget couldn't help herself.

Kaya treated Nugget's safety like a military campaign. She drew maps, set tripwires, and barked orders at a squirrel reconnaissance unit. Finn, by contrast, treated the whole situation like a three-act play. He performed daily entrances, rehearsed rescue speeches, and once hired a parrot choir to sing backup harmonies.

So, when storm clouds rolled in one humid evening, Kaya was already on high alert. She had carved a whole contingency plan into a log labeled *Storm-Based Nugget Extraction Attempts*.

Which, of course, was exactly when Finn made his move.

He appeared in the rain carrying a basket bedazzled with rainbow vines, sequins made from beetle shells, and a single dramatically placed feather.

"This," he whispered, timing his words to the roll of thunder, "will be the most spectacular rescue in jungle history."

He crept toward Nugget's hammock, moving in exaggerated poses that lined up with lightning flashes. Just as his paw brushed the edge of the hammock—

SNAP!

Seven carefully engineered snares tightened at once, yanking him upside down into the air. Finn dangled like a wet ornament, the basket swinging uselessly from his tail. Kaya emerged from the shadows with a smug grin and a steaming thermos of mango smoothie.

"Precipitation-based extraction attempt," she muttered, ticking a box on her paw. "Predicted and neutralized."

"It's not kidnapping!" Finn spun helplessly. "It's artistic rescuing. There's a difference."

"Bedazzling is not rescuing," Kaya said flatly, gesturing to the ridiculously decorated rescue contraption, which had somehow landed upright and was now attracting confused fireflies.

"It's not bedazzled; it's embellished! There's a difference."

"What's the difference?"

"Bedazzling is tacky. Embellishment is *artistic*."

From her hammock, Nugget gave an unimpressed cluck. "Will you both ever get bored of fighting, or is this eternal entertainment for you?"

Both cubs opened their mouths to answer—then froze when Nugget added casually: "Careful. The storm's going to knock that tree over."

They turned. A second later, lightning struck a palm in the distance. The tree split, falling with a crash.

"Lucky guess," Kaya muttered.

"Or intuition," Finn breathed, wide-eyed.

"Or maybe," Nugget said, "I just saw how the wind was pushing it."

She went back to sipping rainwater off a leaf, pretending she wasn't shaken by her own words.

That night, Nugget dreamed. Golden eggs rained from the sky. Voices whispered her name. She woke with her feathers ruffled.

The next morning, as Kaya and Finn argued about whether her breakfast should be served on a banana leaf or a hollowed-out coconut, Nugget interrupted.

"Weird dream last night," she clucked. "Golden eggs. Animals bowing. Very strange."

"Dreams are just brain clutter," Kaya said.

"Or visions of destiny," Finn countered.

"Or maybe I just ate a bad beetle," Nugget retorted.

But the dream clung to her like dew on feathers.

Signs and Portents

The dream lingered the next morning like a stubborn feather stuck to Nugget's wing. She shook herself in her hammock, but the image of golden eggs raining from the sky wouldn't leave.

Kaya was busy arranging berries in perfect pentagon shapes, while Finn practiced his casual lean against a log, tilting his head at just the right angle.

Everything felt ridiculous. Perfectly them—until a finch landed nearby, chattering nervously about whether to move her nest.

"Shift it higher," Nugget said, almost without thinking. "The rains will come in three or four days."

The finch blinked. "How do you know?"

"I don't," Nugget scratched her cowlick. "But the leaves are turning their backs to the wind, the air smells heavy… and my feathers feel twitchy."

The finch flew off, muttering. Kaya snorted. "Nonsense." Finn, on the other paw, gasped as though Nugget had just parted the clouds.

Three days later, the rains came—exactly as she had said.

Word spread. By the time the sun returned, animals were trickling toward Nugget's hammock, curious about the chicken who seemed to know things.

At first, she didn't take it seriously. When two chipmunks arrived squabbling over acorns, Nugget tilted her head and clucked: "Split them. Half for you, half for him. And bury a few so you'll both forget where they are." The chipmunks stopped arguing, stunned.

When a frog fretted over whether to move lily pads, Nugget shrugged: "Try the bigger one. Looks sturdier." Sure enough, the old one sank the next day.

Nugget's advice ranged from obvious to absurd. But somehow, they kept being right. When the chipmunks stopped fighting and the frog's new lily pad didn't sink, the jungle decided she knew things.

Then the golden feathers appeared.

Three of them lay in Nugget's hammock, gleaming as if spun from sunlight.

"Weird magic chicken stuff," whispered a possum.

"Suspicious," said the tortoise. "Could be Finn planting props again."

"How dare you!" Finn clutched his chest. "I would never tamper with sacred poultry destiny."

Kaya pawed through the leaves. "They probably blew in from some exotic bird. Or molted from a parrot. Or..." She trailed off, though her tail lashed with irritation.

Nugget herself wasn't sure. She lifted one feather gingerly. It shimmered in a way that didn't feel normal, though she said out loud: "Maybe someone's prank."

No one believed her. The crowd leaned closer, eyes wide. "Her cowlick," a parrot said. "What if she's the blessed one?"

By evening, Nugget's hammock had become a consultation booth. Animals lined up to ask her advice: what to eat, where to dig, how to calm an angry mate. Nugget tried to keep her answers practical, but every word seemed to land with prophetic weight.

Kaya rolled her eyes. "You're all acting like a chicken can see the future. She's just... irritatingly observant."

Finn was already rehearsing dramatic speeches. "Destiny calls! The legends unfold! All hail the cowlicked one!"

From the edge of the gathering, strangers watched—scouts and travelers who had come just to see "the remarkable chicken." Her morning squabbles with the tigers suddenly felt small compared to this new mystique.

"The gathering," one scout said. "If she truly has the gift, let her demonstrate before all the animals. Let the stories be tested."

Excitement rippled through the assembly. Tales of such gatherings were legendary—events that drew creatures from across the jungle.

"I haven't agreed to any gathering," Nugget said, though her heart thudded with anticipation.

"But you will," the scout replied confidently. "The marked ones always answer destiny's call."

"Or maybe," Kaya said with brutal honesty. "They just enjoy the attention."

Nugget shot her a look but didn't deny it. Once, she had fled a coop to avoid becoming soup. Now, animals were bowing because her feathers stuck up funny.

And though she tried to shake it off, she couldn't ignore a small, unsettling thought: what if there really was something bigger at play?

That night, after the crowds dispersed and gifts were catalogued, Nugget adjusted the flower crown that Finn had somehow convinced her to wear daily.

"You know," she said to Kaya and Finn, "whether or not any of this is real, I have to admit—I'm enjoying myself."

"Adoration has its appeal," Finn agreed. "Though I'm jealous of your golden feather situation. Very dramatic."

"It's probably a coincidence," Kaya said. "Animals look for explanations where none exist."

"As long as I don't start believing my own publicity," Nugget said. She hesitated. "Though... what if some of it is real? What if I really am different?"

The question lingered in the quiet. None of them had an answer.

Unseen by them, in the shadows of the old banyan tree, a pair of eyes watched her newfound influence with mixed feelings. The observer made notes in a worn journal: *Subjects gathering daily. Predictions interpreted as prophecy. Influence expanding beyond immediate circle.*

He paused, then crossed out the last line.

Above them all, the jungle held its breath. And in her hammock, Nugget dreamed of golden eggs and ancient voices calling her name.

The Talent Showdown

The clearing near the watering hole had never seen such excitement. Word of the Great Tiger Showdown spread like gossip through the jungle grapevine.

Three days earlier—two weeks after Nugget's oddly specific rain prediction had come true—fed up with Kaya and Finn's constant bickering and increasingly elaborate schemes, Nugget had finally put her foot—er, claw—down.

Nugget fluffed her feathers in annoyance. "Enough! You two want to prove who's the better protector? Fine. Let's settle this properly, once and for all. A competition. Winner gets... bragging rights, I guess. But this ridiculous war ends today."

Now, three days later, animals flocked from throughout the jungle to see the notorious frenemies compete in an official contest to determine Nugget's ultimate protector. Sure, there were whispers about Nugget's recent... unusual behavior. The rain thing was weird. And there was something different in her eyes lately. But mostly, everyone was just excited to see which tiger would emerge victorious.

"My berries are on the striped one," The squirrel clutched its acorns tighter.

"Which one? They're both striped," replied a confused armadillo.

"The... stripier one?"

Nugget perched on her flower-decorated perch, looking every inch the center of attention, though she occasionally tilted her head like she was listening to something only she could hear. The tigers were preparing for days; each convinced his approach would finally prove his superiority.

This was their moment. The moment that would settle, once and for all, who was the better tiger.

At the front, perched on a raised log smothered in moss and poorly chosen glitter, sat the judges: a toucan with a monocle who kept polishing it obsessively, a perpetually unimpressed tapir munching lazily on moss clumps, and a lemur vibrating with joy, already applauding absolutely everything.

Nugget was adjusting the angle of her coconut juice when a low bow from the edge of the crowd caught her eye.

A sloth descended from the canopy with ceremonial slowness, each movement deliberate and weighted with purpose. It touched the ground and continued lowering until its belly nearly scraped the earth, massive claws spread wide like an offering. Its ancient eyes never left Nugget's face.

"Your Highness," the sloth whispered.

"Excuse me?" Nugget clucked.

The sloth nodded. "Forgive the delay. We don't move fast. But my family has followed the Cowlick Star for generations. We knew you'd come."

Nugget stared. "Did you just call me... a star?"

"The crowned one. The Unplucked. The Chosen Chick."

Nugget's eyes widened. "That's... a lot of titles. Are you sure you've got the right chicken?"

But the sloth was already curling into a meditation pose, mumbling something about "beaked balance" and "feathered fulfillment."

A puzzled Nugget reclined on her floral perch, a regal nest of banana leaves and delusion, and took a long sip of the coconut juice from the bamboo straw. She then gave a languid wave of one wing. "Begin." Nugget spread her wings slightly, a glint of mischief in her eyes.

With a sudden *whoosh*, Kaya made her entrance, swinging in on a vine like she was born for Broadway, flinging handfuls of shimmering jungle petals into the air. The crowd gasped. She landed in a crouch, rolled, and launched into what she dubbed "The Chicken and the Storm," an interpretive dance of loyalty, destiny, and, apparently, weather systems.

She leapt. She twirled. She created a jungle storm out of shadow puppets, danced through imaginary lightning, and capped it off by diving behind a massive papier-mâché egg... only to burst out of it seconds later in a slow-motion roar, feathers flying and vines erupting in a confetti blast. Somewhere in the crowd, a squirrel dropped its acorn in shock and then pretended it meant to do that. The lemur was crying.

Kaya's movements mirrored the storm Nugget had predicted days before. A capuchin monkey leaned toward its neighbor and whispered, "She moves like the rain that came exactly when the chicken said it would."

As Kaya left the stage, she shot Finn a sideways glance. "Style points count, Finn," she said with a hint of smugness, "even when the style is backed by an eighteen-step plan."

From her throne, Nugget watched with that new, distant look in her eyes, occasionally tilting her head as if listening to music only she could hear. Her gaze followed Kaya's storm dance with an intensity that made several animals shift uncomfortably—like she was seeing more than just the performance.

As the petals settled, Kaya struck a final pose with her head high, claws out, tail curved in an artful swoop. Nugget gave a small, neutral nod. Kaya's eyes flicked to Finn, daring him to top that.

"Prepare to be *cluckstruck*," Finn declared, stepping onto the stage with the air of someone who had vague plans involving sparkly explosions and complete confidence in his improvisation skills. He wore a leafy cape, which he promptly flung behind him like a drama king.

He began by juggling three armadillos, each one seemingly enjoying the show and waving at the crowd. Then came plate-spinning, with carved bark dishes twirling on sharpened sticks. The frogs entered next, forming a synchronized chorus line that danced to a jungle-funk rhythm while Finn beatboxed flawlessly. The lemur began clapping in time. The monkeys went wild. A civet fainted.

For the grand finale, Finn unveiled a questionable contraption built from fermented fruit, dry moss, and something that looked suspiciously like honey badger fur. He struck a pose, lit the fuse, and waited.

BOOM.

A tree burst into flames.

As the sparks settled and smoke cleared from Finn's explosive finale, Nugget murmured something under her breath that only the nearest animals could catch: "Fire and spectacle... just like the old stories tell."

A young lemur tugged on its mother's arm. "Mama, do you think she knew that would happen?"

The mother lemur glanced at Nugget, who was now staring at the smoldering tree with an expression of vague recognition, as if she had seen this exact scene before. "I don't know, little one. But I'm starting to wonder how much that chicken really sees."

The audience screamed, then cheered. The lemur was on their feet, throwing flowers. The toucan dabbed away tears with a leaf napkin. The tapir did not blink.

As the last sparks faded, Finn bowed with a flourish and mouthed, *"You're welcome."* A raccoon snatched his discarded cape and ran off, yelling, "I'M FINN NOW!"

From her perch, Nugget gave her coconut juice a slow swirl. "So much effort," she said, not entirely to herself. "So little dignity. I love it." She plucked up a peeled lychee, snapped it down, and nestled deeper into her nest. "Next event better have snacks."

The judges huddled to discuss their scores. Nugget rose gracefully from her seat and approached the edge of her platform. The crowd fell silent, expecting her to comment on the performances.

Instead, she gazed out at the assembled animals with those increasingly mysterious eyes and spoke in a voice that carried further than it should have: "Sometimes the best performance is the one that surprises even the performer. True artistry comes not from planning every step, but from dancing with the unexpected."

The words hung in the air like morning mist. Murmurs rippled through the crowd—was the chicken being philosophical, or was there something deeper in those carefully chosen words? Even Kaya and Finn, still panting from their performances, felt like Nugget was talking about more than just their talent show.

The toucan adjusted his monocle nervously. "Quite... quite profound."

Nugget blinked, looking suddenly confused by her own words. "Oh. Yes. Well. Anyway, let's see those scores, shall we?"

The judges muttered, scribbled, and finally held up their scores. The toucan gave Kaya a 9 and Finn a 10. The lemur screamed "TEN!" for both and added a flower to each scorecard. The tapir, true to form, gave everyone a 3 and went back to chewing moss.

Kaya and Finn stood side by side, panting slightly, petals and soot clinging to their fur. They did not speak. Their eyes said everything: *this isn't over.*

Nugget, still lounging, adjusted her cowlick and smiled. "This," she whispered to no one in particular, "is better than the best soap opera out there."

Mic Drop at Sunset

The sun dipped low, casting a golden glow over the jungle clearing where a circle of animals gathered, buzzing with anticipation. Fireflies blinked on and off, like tiny spotlights, setting the stage for the most unexpected showdown of the season: the Jungle Rap Battle.

Nugget perched high on a twisted banyan branch, her eyes sparkling with amusement. This was her favorite kind of drama—just enough chaos to keep things spicy without any real harm. Though lately, she'd been feeling... different. The golden feather she found clutched in her claw this morning still puzzled her. Where did it come from?

The crowd was a wild mix: chatty monkeys, a curious pangolin, a couple of wide-eyed parrots, and, of course, the distinguished judges. The toucan was adjusting his monocle with serious intent, the tapir wore his usual "resting judge-face", and the lemur was just happy to be here, occasionally clapping like a fan at a concert.

After yesterday's talent show—here Nugget had spoken with unexpected wisdom about art and destiny—animals were watching her more intently than usual. Some hoped she might predict today's winner. Others whispered about her strange comments that seemed to mean more than they should.

Kaya stepped forward first, her stripes blazing in the sunset light. She cleared her throat, then launched into her verse with fierce confidence:

"Yo, I'm the Queen of the scene with the claws so clean,
Got stripes so bright, I make the jungle beam!
Ancient patterns in my stride,
Golden futures I can't hide,
Protectin' Nugget like she's gold on a throne,
Stripes of destiny, secrets the jungle's known!"

Her voice was sharp and rhythmic; every word was delivered with precision. But as the last lines left her mouth, Kaya faltered slightly. What did she just sing? She meant to brag about her planning skills, but somehow "ancient patterns" and "golden futures" spilled out instead.

The monkeys hooted in approval, the parrots nodded along, and even the tapir raised an eyebrow, momentarily interested.

Finn paced at the edge of the circle, muttering to himself. "Alright, breathe... remember the rhymes, hit the beat on the third log thump, and pause for the lemur's applause. This is strategy. I'm doing strategy. With style, obviously."

Finn bounced into the circle next; a cocky grin plastered on his face. He wiggled his tail. "Alright, time to bring the heat," and then spat his verse with swagger:

"I'm the king of stealth,
Got that predator wealth,
Legends written in the stars,
Crowns and kingdoms, near and far,
Sneakin' through shadows, protectin' Nugget's health,
But right here's where power's shown,
Guarding what we call our own!"

His delivery was full of bravado, his tail flicking in rhythm, but like Kaya, he felt a moment of confusion. "Legends written in the stars"? "Crowns and kingdoms"? Those weren't the boastful lyrics he planned.

A strange hush fell over the crowd as the last echoes of their verses faded. The lyrics started as typical boasting, but something about those final lines felt... significant. "Crowns and kingdoms," "legends written in the stars"—really?

A murmur ran through the assembled animals like wind through leaves. Several creatures glanced nervously at Nugget, who was staring at the tigers with an unreadable expression, her head tilted as if she was hearing an echo of something important.

"Did they just..." whispered a parrot to its neighbor.

"Probably a fluke." The monkey scratched its head, eyes darting nervously. "Right? Just... rhyming words that sounded good?"

But the words hung in the air like morning mist, and everyone could feel that something shifted. Even Kaya and Finn exchanged uncertain glances—where did those phrases come from?

As the battle heated up with more conventional verses, the audience became totally engaged. Monkeys were beat boxing on hollow logs, a baby jaguar was bouncing in excitement, and even the usually stoic tapir found himself tapping his hooves to the beat. The jungle was alive with energy and laughter.

But the mysterious lyrics lingered in everyone's minds.

Just as Finn finished his final verse with an animated roar, Nugget rose slowly from her branch, her movements more deliberate than usual.

"Congratulations, you've invented the world's first self-fulfilling prophecy: rhyme badly enough, and the jungle will believe you," she sighed.

The clearing fell completely silent. Even the fireflies seemed to dim their blinking.

Nugget blinked suddenly, looking surprised by her own words. "I mean... good job with the rhyming, you two. Very... rhythmic."

But the damage was done. Every animal in the clearing was now staring at her with a mixture of awe and uncertainty.

The lemur threw himself onto the forest floor like an actor auditioning for "Most Tragic Jungle Moment."

The toucan dabbed at his eyes with a tiny jungle leaf, muttering, "Too much talent in one place... or perhaps something more."

The tapir, ever the traditionalist, sighed deeply and gave both tigers a 3, mumbling something about "maintaining judge dignity in supernatural circumstances."

Nugget, seemingly recovered from her mysterious moment, fluttered down from her branch, clucking with nervous laughter. "You two might not settle the score today, but I'm thoroughly entertained." Nugget brushed a stray feather from her crown—the same golden color as the mysterious feather from this morning.

The jungle echoed with cheers and applause as the fireflies flared brighter, but underneath the celebration, an undercurrent of whispers flowed through the crowd. Something was definitely happening to the cute chicken, and tomorrow's final competition promised to be more than just a simple obstacle course.

Deep in the undergrowth, a pair of civets whispered beneath a cluster of fern leaves.

One twitched his whiskers. "You'd seen the chicken lately?"

"You mean Queen Featherpants?" the other snorted. "She just declared Wednesday as 'No Pecking Without Consent Day.'"

"She made the tapir do a bow. A full bow."

"It's starting to get weird," the first civet said. "The tigers keep showing off, the monkeys won't stop singing her name, and now my kids are making stick-thrones for their plush toys. Plus, did you hear what she said about prophecies?"

The second civet shifted on its paws. "I heard. My cousin had a dream about golden eggs last night. Woke up bowing to our rooster."

From the shadows, a scarred boar listened, eyes narrowed. "This jungle's gone soft," he growled, and vanished into the underbrush.

That night, as the jungle settled into its evening chorus, something unprecedented happened. Three different animals—a family of opossums, an elderly tortoise, and a young jaguar—independently experienced the same vivid dream.

In the dream, golden eggs rained from the sky while a voice like distant thunder spoke of crowns made of feathers and destiny written in cowlicks. They saw tigers with stripes that glowed like starlight, protecting something precious that would change everything.

All three woke at the exact moment, just before dawn, with the strange compulsion to bow whenever they saw chickens. None of them could remember why.

Elsewhere, in her hammock between the tiger territories, Nugget tossed and turned, dreaming not of golden eggs but of ancient voices calling her name and a weight settling on her head that felt remarkably like a crown.

She woke with three golden feathers clutched in her claws—feathers that certainly hadn't been there when she went to sleep, and which matched the one from yesterday morning perfectly.

Tigers on Trail

The morning of the final event dawned humid and thick with jungle anticipation, but underneath the familiar buzz of excitement lay something else entirely—a tension that made every leaf seem to whisper secrets.

News traveled fast: the last challenge was a grueling obstacle course designed by Nugget herself, and after yesterday's mysterious rap battle, every animal in the jungle wanted to see what would happen next.

Nugget woke up with five golden feathers clutched in her claws. Five. Each morning brought more, and she had no idea why. The weight of them felt significant, like breadcrumbs leading to something she couldn't yet see. She tucked them carefully into her crown, where they caught the morning light like tiny suns.

The clearing was converted into a chaotic playground of mud pits, swinging vines, rolling logs, and a surprisingly grouchy troop of porcupines who eyed the contestants with visible disdain. Nearby, a honey badger watched with a puzzled expression, clearly wondering what all the fuss was about.

But this audience was different from the previous games. Animals whispered excitedly about yesterday's strange lyrics and Nugget's cryptic comments about prophecies. Several creatures experienced vivid dreams of golden eggs and feathered crowns. The tension in the air was palpable—everyone sensed that today would bring answers to questions they were only beginning to understand.

Nugget perched at the top of the slippery slope, wings crossed, and a complex expression on her face. The golden feathers in her crown seemed to shimmer with their own light, and her eyes held that distant look that became increasingly frequent.

"Let's see who's really got what it takes," she said. The words seemed to mean more than just the obstacle course ahead.

The audience was buzzing with nervous energy. Parrots squawked excitedly from the treetops, monkeys swung overhead chattering bets, and the ever-dignified tapir sat on a log with his eyes sharp behind his spectacles. The toucan with his monocle, with a slow nod, while the lemur bounced in place, barely containing his excitement.

"Think she'll do it again?" whispered a capuchin monkey. "Say something... mysterious?"

"After yesterday?" replied its neighbor. "I'd be surprised if she didn't."

With a flash of determination, Kaya launched herself forward, muscles rippling as she dove into the first mud pit, splattering mud like a pro. Her movements were precise, calculated—every leap and bound part of a carefully planned strategy. She swung gracefully from vine to vine, her movements a blur of power and precision.

But as she moved through the course, something strange happened. Her route began to mirror patterns she never planned—ancient symbols, geometric designs that seemed to flow from some deeper knowledge. Animals watching gasped as they recognized the shapes: spirals of destiny, the dance of the storm-bringer, movements that belonged in old stories rather than obstacle courses.

Finn stalked behind with calculated stealth, eyes sharp as he tackled the rolling logs, sidestepping the porcupines with a quick flick of his paw. The porcupines bristled, but Finn's nimble footwork saved him from a prickly situation.

Yet, he too found himself moving in ways he never practiced. His leaps became more flamboyant, more ceremonial—like a ritual dance passed down through generations. His poses between obstacles resembled those of ancient guardians, protectors of sacred things.

"They're not just running a course," said the wise old tortoise who'd had prophetic dreams. "They're performing the old ceremonies. Look at their patterns."

Then came the chaos: Kaya got caught in one of her own vine traps! She yelped in surprise as the vines wrapped around her, hoisting her off the ground like jungle spaghetti. But even trapped, her struggles traced the air in meaningful arcs.

Kaya twisted free with an unscripted spin that landed her upright. She allowed herself a sly grin.

"Sometimes, Finn, you've got to improvise with style. And yes, I said *style*."

Finn grinned and surged ahead, taking the lead, his movements becoming increasingly graceful and purposeful.

But the final hurdle awaited: the slick, steep slope where Nugget stood like a final guardian, wings on hips.

Both tigers scrambled upward, claws digging for grip. Breaths came ragged as they neared the top. The crowd held its breath. This was it—the moment that would determine the ultimate winner.

Then, thud! They collided mid-leap, tumbling down in a furry, growling heap.

Kaya and Finn rolled down the slope in a tangle of fur and frustrated growls. For a brief moment, Nugget felt dizzy—probably the afternoon heat and stress. Her eyes went wide, unfocused. The words that came out sounded important, though she wasn't sure what they meant:

"When stripes unite and fall as one,
The jungle's greatest test has begun.
Not victory, but harmony,
Shall crack the shell of destiny!"

The words echoed through the clearing like thunder, and as they faded, a golden light seemed to emanate from Nugget herself—though this was almost certainly just the afternoon sun hitting her at a particularly flattering angle. She blinked, confused by her own babbling. Around her, gasps rippled through the crowd like she'd just revealed the secrets of the universe.

The rolling tigers stopped mid-tumble, staring up at Nugget in wonder and confusion.

"The prophecy," breathed the ancient tortoise who had witnessed seven different jungle regimes declare themselves chosen by destiny. "Number eight begins."

Nugget blinked, the glow fading, looking as shocked as everyone else. "Did I just... what did I just say?" She touched the golden feathers in her crown with trembling claws. "And why are these things glowing?"

The judges forgot to announce scores. The audience forgot to cheer. Everyone was staring at Nugget, who looked as surprised as anyone. The air itself seemed different now, charged with possibility and ancient power.

"That sounded…" the toucan began, his monocle fogging with excitement.

"Like prophecy," finished the tapir, his usual boredom replaced by unmistakable awe.

Kaya and Finn, still covered in mud and vines, stared at each other across the clearing. Finn's eyes were wide with wonder—this was exactly the kind of mystical validation he'd always hoped for. Kaya's expression was more complicated: part amazement at what she'd witnessed, part analytical mind trying to find rational explanations, and part growing suspicion that maybe her instincts about Nugget had been more accurate than her logic wanted to admit.

From the crowd, a mysterious mongoose emerged, slipping closer through the shadows as he quickly sketched symbols in a small notebook. He'd been watching, waiting for something—though whether he'd expected this particular moment was unclear from his stoic expression.

With the scores forgotten and the competition transcended, Nugget cleared her throat dramatically, though her voice shook slightly.

"Looks like we have more than just a tie." Her gaze swept over the reverent crowd. "I think... I think we have the beginning of something none of us quite understands yet."

The tigers, for once in perfect agreement, nodded slowly. Whatever game they've been playing, it just became something much bigger.

Nugget gave a small, wry shake of her head. "Joint custody champions. And apparently... I'm something more than just your referee."

Later, after the crowd dispersed in hushed, excited whispers, Nugget pulled her friends aside. The golden feathers in her crown had stopped glowing but still radiated warmth.

"That thing I said up there," she whispered, her feathers ruffled with concern and wonder. "It just...

happened. Like someone else was speaking through me."

"The words felt..." Kaya paused, her analytical mind wrestling with what she'd witnessed. "Significant. But words can feel important when animals are staring at you expectantly."

"And our movements during the course," Finn added. "I've never trained to move like that, but it felt... right. Ancient."

"Muscle memory from watching other animals," Kaya said, though her voice lacked conviction. "Or instinctive responses to pressure situations."

Finn was convinced something mystical was happening, Nugget was confused by her own experience, and Kaya was struggling between rational explanations and the growing evidence that her logical frameworks might be inadequate.

And in the gathering dusk, as fireflies began their evening dance, the jungle itself seemed to exhale—as if it was holding its breath for a very long time, waiting for this moment when destiny finally announced itself.

The golden feathers in Nugget's crown caught the last rays of sunlight, and for just a moment, they looked remarkably like a crown.

"We need answers," Kaya said finally. "That prophecy, those movements we made, these glowing feathers—there has to be a logical explanation for all of this."

"Any explanation would be nice," Finn added. "Rational, mystical, or just really weird coincidence."

Nugget touched the flowers in her crown thoughtfully. "Well, whatever's happening, at least I'm getting better at impromptu poetry. That's a marketable skill, right?"

"We find out what it all means," she continued. "Tomorrow. First thing. And we find rational explanations."

Nugget was exasperated and slightly hoarse from cheering, but her decision was final. "I'm moving into a hammock suspended between your territories."

The tigers now had joint custody along with a shared schedule (carved into tree bark) to manage visits.

But none of them slept well that night. And when morning came, Nugget was gone.

Cluck of Shadows

It began at dawn with an empty hammock and three golden feathers scattered on the ground below.

Kaya discovered the absence first. She'd come early with breakfast—a collection of plump, juicy worms arranged in a perfect spiral pattern she knew Nugget would appreciate—and found only swaying rope and the lingering scent of something she couldn't identify, something that reminded her of old stones and forgotten places.

The golden feathers lay where they had fallen, no longer glowing but still warm to the touch, as if they remembered the strange words that had flowed through them just hours before.

"FINN!" Kaya's roar echoed through the jungle, panic sharpening her voice.

He arrived in seconds, took one look at the empty hammock, and felt his stomach drop. "She wouldn't just leave. Not after what happened yesterday. Not after... whatever that was she said."

"Look." Kaya pointed to the feathers. "She left these behind. Or... they fell off when she..." She couldn't finish the thought.

But then Finn's sharp eyes caught something else—a trail of disturbed earth leading away from the clearing, and there, pressed into the soft mud near the hammock's base, the clear print of a clawed foot. Too large to be Nugget's. Too deliberate to be accidental.

"She didn't leave," Finn growled, his protective instincts flaring. "Someone took her."

A single feather, delicately curled and golden, marked the beginning of their trail.

Kaya and Finn followed the sparse clues with the flair of detectives who had absolutely no training for detective work. They tracked feathers that seemed to appear just when they needed them most, footprints that led in purposeful directions, and the occasional half-eaten worm that suggested Nugget had passed this way.

Their investigation led them to interrogate the local monkeys, who responded by performing interpretive dances that conveyed exactly nothing useful. The parakeet choir provided what they claimed was a dramatic reenactment of Nugget being carried away by a mysterious figure, complete with synchronized squawking and aerial choreography.

"You swear you saw this happen?" Kaya demanded.

"Well... no," admitted the lead parakeet. "But Larry here had a very vivid dream about it. We thought the reenactment might help."

"Dreams are not evidence," Finn sputtered.

"Tell that to the prophecy," Larry muttered under his breath.

Following the trail deeper into the jungle, Kaya and Finn found themselves approaching a place neither had dared enter before: The Whispering Grove.

An eerie hush hung over the ancient trees, the usual hum of insects replaced by a soft rustling that sounded almost like voices murmuring secrets just beyond understanding. Even the boldest jungle creatures avoided this place, though none could say exactly why.

"This place gives me the creeps." Finn's ears twitched at every shadow.

Kaya sniffed the air, detecting layers of scent that spoke of great age and deeper mysteries. "This is where the elders used to come, before our time. I heard tales... about jungle truths hidden in leaves and stones."

At the grove's center stood an ancient banyan tree, its massive roots twisted like gnarled claws around a weathered stone tablet. Moss and vines had nearly claimed the monument, but underneath, Kaya could see the faint traces of deliberate carving.

She brushed away centuries of growth, revealing script that seemed to pulse with its significance.

Finn squinted at the markings. "What does it say?"

Kaya's scholarly instincts took over. "Let me try." She read aloud, slowly deciphering the jagged script that seemed to shift and change as she looked at it:

"When might makes bitter right,
One born of fluff shall rise,
A cowlicked queen of earth and sky,
To unify claw and beak with wit, not war."

Finn blinked hard. "Cowlicked... Queen?"

They stared at each other as different realizations dawned.

Kaya's voice was barely a whisper. "Remember what we talked about? After the storm? About our instincts telling us something was different about her?"

Finn nodded slowly, eyes wide with wonder. "The prophecy... it was always about her."

Kaya adjusted her feathers, her analytical mind kicking in. "Or we've been unconsciously drawn to someone with natural leadership abilities, and now we're retrofitting ancient poetry to explain our good instincts about character."

"But the cowlick—" Finn started.

"Half the animals in this jungle have cowlicks if you look hard enough." The confidence in Kaya's voice wavered. "Ancient prophecies have a way of... fitting whatever people need them to fit."

The Mongoose Reveals Himself

A rustling came from the hollow banyan and out stepped a small figure adjusting a glinting monocle. The mongoose's tiny trench coat—where had he even found such a thing? —billowed around him as if caught in a phantom breeze, though not a single leaf stirred on the trees around them.

"I see you've found the old prophecy." Clive emerged from shadows that seemed deeper than they should be. His small satchel clinked softly—too softly, as if he trained himself to move quietly. "Interesting timing, that."

"I've been tracking your movements for some time. Force of habit—I used to make quite a living knowing where everyone was and what they were doing."

Finn's fur bristled with recognition. "You! You were watching us, weren't you? Taking notes about everything we did?"

The mongoose tilted his head, unsurprised by their recognition. "Observant of you. Yes, I've been monitoring the situation for some time now."

Kaya stepped forward, her instincts finally making sense. "You've been watching more than just us, haven't you?"

Clive adjusted his monocle. "Information gathering is an old habit. I've always found it useful to... know things before others do."

"Your instincts were entirely correct," Clive confirmed with a slight smile. "Though I suspect you both thought you were going mad at times."

He approached the ancient stone with the casual authority of someone who possessed credentials somewhere, even if no one was quite sure where. "This," he continued, tapping the worn tablet with one small claw, "is one of the original Cluckscroll inscriptions. Translated by beetle monks. Possibly chickens. The historical records are... interpretive."

Finn shook his head, still processing the magnitude of what they discovered. "So, when we said there was something special about her..."

"You were recognizing something," Clive replied with professional neutrality. "Whether that's natural leadership ability, destiny, or just two young predators getting attached to an unusual situation... well, that depends on which explanation serves your purposes."

Kaya's claws traced the ancient markings with growing suspicion. "Wait... you actually believe this prophecy stuff?"

Clive shrugged with practiced ambiguity. "I believe prophecies work exactly as well as people need them to work. Which is to say: roughly forty percent history, forty percent educated guesswork, and twenty percent interpretive dance."

He pointed to specific etchings on the stone. "This section here translates as 'When stripes clash and feathers flare, one shall rise with beak and flair.' Though it might be 'fire' instead of 'flair.' Ancient translations can be... challenging."

Finn raised an eyebrow. "So... she's the chosen chicken?"

"She's a chicken who's created an interesting situation," Clive said. "Whether through competence, luck, timing, or cosmic intervention... that's above my pay grade."

As the tigers absorbed this revelation, Clive's eyes moved methodically across the grove, cataloguing escape routes and noting which animals had gathered at the edges to listen. His paw moved almost unconsciously, sketching symbols in the dirt that looked remarkably like a code. When Kaya's sharp eyes caught the movement, Clive smoothly brushed the marks away. "Just noting the translation." He smiled, but the warmth never reached his eyes.

"The Cowlick Crown," Clive said, studying the ancient markings. "Apparently, it's significant. Though I suspect its significance depends largely on who's doing the interpreting."

"Either way," Clive continued, "it is more than just an amusing hairstyle. Maybe it's a symbol. Of balance. Of the absurd becoming profound."

Kaya muttered, "This entire jungle has lost its mind."

"Quite possibly," Clive replied cheerfully, "though your friend might be exactly the right kind of practical to navigate that particular form of madness."

"Who are you anyway?" Kaya growled, though with considerably less hostility than before. Their recent revelations had prepared them for strangeness.

"My identity is relatively unimportant." He made a casual, dismissive gesture with his paw. "But since you seem to require credentials, I am Clive, field agent for the Cluckspiracy Bureau. What matters more is your relationship to prophecies. You see, they're tricky things. They only hold power when someone believes in them. The question is: do you?"

The tigers felt that familiar moment of shared understanding—the same feeling from that night after the storm, when they first admitted something was different about their friend.

Finn nodded slowly. "Our instincts led us this far. If she really is the one the prophecy speaks of... we must find her."

Kaya set her jaw with characteristic determination. "And make sure no one with darker intentions finds her first."

"Excellent." Clive produced a small notebook from his coat. "As it happens, I've located her current position."

"Where?" Kaya demanded.

Clive polished his monocle, then held it up to the light as though weighing an idea. "That information will cost you three beetles and a professional drumroll."

Finn rolled his eyes but obligingly banged his paw against a nearby tree trunk. Clive nodded with satisfaction.

"She was last seen heading toward the abandoned spice grove... in the company of a rather militant band of Jungle Hens."

The Poultry Revolution

The tigers burst into the overgrown spice grove, where the air hung heavy with the scents of cardamom, rebellion, and what could only be described as an organized poultry uprising.

There, elevated on a throne constructed entirely of coconuts and delusions of grandeur, sat Nugget. She held a carved wooden staff topped with chicken feathers and wore an expression of serene authority that suggested she had found her true calling.

Around her, a devoted flock of Jungle Hens gazed up with the fervor of newly converted disciples.

"HELLO, STRANGERS," Nugget's voice carried farther than it ever had. "Welcome to the liberation."

"What... exactly is happening here?" Finn whispered, taking in the scene with bewildered fascination.

Kaya narrowed her eyes, watching the hens organize themselves into what appeared to be military formations. "Apparently, she's leading some kind of poultry revolution."

Nugget, noting their confusion, graciously explained her situation. She had grown weary of being fought over like a prized jungle ornament, she said. In seeking solitude to understand the strange things happening to her, she stumbled upon a gathering of hens discussing their lack of representation in jungle leadership. One thing had led to another, and before she knew it, she accidentally founded a chicken empowerment movement.

The hens, it seemed, had no intention of leaving.

They had taken to calling her 'The Beaked One.'

"She taught us confidence," proclaimed one hen.

"She taught us how to roost with pride," clucked another, demonstrating a roosting technique that somehow conveyed fierce dignity.

"She taught us self-defense using beak-jitsu," squawked a third, executing what appeared to be a martial arts kata with her beak.

Kaya rubbed her temples, feeling a headache forming. "We just came to bring you breakfast worms."

Nugget sniffed with newfound authority. "Well, perhaps I'm tired of being treated like a snack or a sidekick. Maybe... I'm ready to be the main course."

Finn blinked. "That sounded considerably more threatening than you probably intended."

"I meant it metaphorically," Nugget clarified hastily.

Feathers and Fisticuffs

Just as the tigers were processing this new development, a commotion erupted at the grove's entrance. A large, imposing rooster named Big Cluck strode in, his feathers flaring with territorial aggression.

"There's only room for one leader in this grove," he bellowed, fixing Nugget with a challenging stare.

The hens gasped in collective dismay. This was clearly a situation they had been dreading.

Finn and Kaya moved to intervene, but Nugget held up a wing with calm authority. "I've got this under control."

Big Cluck puffed out his chest and issued his challenge: a formal duel to determine rightful leadership of the grove.

The hens fell silent, waiting to see how their newly crowned leader would respond.

"Accepted," Nugget said simply. "What type of duel did you have in mind?"

Big Cluck's beak curved in a superior smile. "A jungle trivia contest. First to miss a question loses everything."

"Question One!" he bellowed with theatrical flair. "What is the capital of Jungle Tree Toad Territory?"

"Blorpington," Nugget's beak didn't pause.

"Correct," Big Cluck admitted grudgingly.

Kaya whispered in amazement, "How could she possibly know that?"

"She reads the informational leaflets the Tree Toad Council drops from the canopy," Finn explained, shaking his head in wonder. "I've seen her studying them during breakfast."

The contest continued through increasingly obscure questions about jungle geography, inter-species treaties, and historical migration patterns. Nugget answered each one with increasing certainty, finally delivering the contest-winning answer"— "Bananaopolis"—with such authoritative flair that the hens erupted in triumphant cheers.

As Big Cluck slunk away in defeat, Nugget resumed her position on the coconut throne with the satisfaction of someone who'd just proven herself in ways she hadn't known were possible.

As the celebration continued, two geckos basked on a warm rock at the grove's edge, their conversation carrying implications none of the revelers suspected.

"Did you hear what the hornbill reported?" the first gecko asked. His tail flicked in slow arcs.

"What now?" replied its companion.

"Claims a golden egg was spotted right here in the grove. Unhatched. Glowing. Marked with mystical feathers."

"They're saying it's a sign. That the prophecy is manifesting. That the Cowlick Crown's power is growing."

"You geckos will believe anything," muttered a passing squirrel. "Probably just has a beetle stuck inside making it glow."

But in the shadows above, Clive closed his observation notebook and murmured to himself,

"The patterns are accelerating. Whatever this is, it's gaining momentum.

Epilogue

Eventually, Kaya and Finn managed to persuade Nugget to return to her hammock, though only after she negotiated one weekend per month to continue her leadership seminars for the hens.

As they walked back through the jungle, Nugget adjusted the ceremonial sash the hens had woven for her, which read 'Supreme Henmistress' in carefully pecked letters.

"You know," she mused, "being worshipped by a devoted following isn't quite as glamorous as one might expect. Though I must admit, the foot massages were exceptional."

Both tigers straightened simultaneously.

"I'm designing her a proper throne with paw-shaped cushions," Finn said.

"Maybe we should commission the parrots to compose an official theme song," Kaya countered.

Nugget grinned with the satisfaction of someone who'd discovered hidden depths within herself. "And you both insisted jungle politics were boring."

Later, those passing the abandoned spice grove swore a faint glow lingered where Nugget's coconut throne had stood—though whether it was real or only imagined, no one could say.

The Crowning Reluctance

The morning after the prophecy revelation brought visitors—lots of them.

Nugget woke to find her hammock surrounded by a nervous delegation of animals, each clutching small offerings and wearing expressions that suggested they'd been rehearsing speeches since dawn.

"Your Majesty," began a finch. She trembled slightly as she held out a perfectly arranged bouquet of morning flowers. "We've come to formally request—"

"Your Majesty?" Nugget interrupted, one eye still closed. "That's new."

"The prophecy," explained a young capuchin monkey earnestly. "Now that we know you're the Cowlick

Crown the ancient stones foretold... we've been thinking about what it means."

Nugget blinked both eyes open. Memories of Clive's translation flooded back. "The old tablet. 'One born of fluff shall rise.'"

"Your destiny," whispered a badger with obvious reverence. "The golden feathers appearing each morning, the way you predicted that storm, those words that came through you during the games..."

"The cowlick," added a squirrel solemnly, pointing at Nugget's distinctive feather tuft. "Just like the prophecy described."

From behind the delegation, Finn bounded forward with the energy of someone who'd been planning this moment all week.

"Nugget!" His voice carried the excitement of a child who'd discovered the perfect game. "They want to make it official! A proper crowning ceremony! Think about it—flower parades, singing ceremonies, maybe even a royal perch designed specifically for optimal sunbathing!"

"A what ceremony?" Nugget asked, though she found herself sitting up straighter despite her confusion.

"A celebration of your obvious destiny," Finn continued, practically vibrating with enthusiasm. "I've been talking with everyone, and the consensus is overwhelming. You're already solving disputes, coordinating responses, making decisions that affect multiple communities..."

"That just sort of happened—"

"Exactly! Natural leadership manifesting through mystical calling!" Finn began pacing with theatrical flair. "Plus, think of the pageantry possibilities. Royal speeches, ceremonial processions, maybe even a talent show where subjects compete for your favor!"

Despite herself, Nugget felt a flutter of interest. The dreams had been getting more vivid lately—golden eggs, ancient voices calling her name, that strange sense of destiny she couldn't quite shake.

"You really think I'm... special?" she asked, preening slightly.

"The special-est," Finn said. "Look at the evidence! The timing of your arrival, the way animals naturally gravitate toward you, the prophetic words that just flow out of you..."

A young monkey bounced forward. "Plus, you make everything more fun! Even territorial disputes become entertaining when you're involved!"

"And you do have that glow about you lately," added a thoughtful beaver. "Like you're lit from within by cosmic chicken energy."

Kaya limped into the clearing, still recovering from the obstacle course injuries, her expression skeptical.

"Can we talk about this rationally for a moment?" she asked, settling carefully beside Nugget's hammock. "A few prophetic-sounding words don't automatically qualify someone for leadership of the entire jungle."

"But the golden feathers—" the finch protested.

"Could be molted from any golden bird," Kaya pointed out pragmatically. "And the storm prediction could have been good weather sense combined with lucky timing."

"What about the way animals naturally follow her?" Finn challenged.

"You share food. You stop fights. Animals remember that." Kaya's voice sharpened with impatience. "Doesn't need magic to explain it."

The delegation's ears drooped slightly, but they pressed closer to Nugget's hammock.

"What about when the food runs short?" Kaya's voice sharpened. "When there's not enough territory for everyone? When you have to choose which animals get what they need?"

Nugget's crest flattened as the questions hit. She hadn't thought past the ceremonies and celebration.

"When animals are hungry and angry, will they still think you're chosen by ancient powers? Or will they remember you're just a chicken who took them for a ride on a couple of lucky coincidences?"

The question hung in the air like morning mist.

Nugget found herself torn between Kaya's practical concerns and the intoxicating possibilities Finn painted.

"Tell me more about this ceremony," she said to the delegation, earning a sharp look from Kaya.

"Well," the finch began excitedly, "we were thinking flower crown presentation at sunrise, followed by tribute offerings from each community, then ceremonial songs about your wisdom and beauty..."

"My beauty?" Nugget preened despite herself.

"The most magnificent cowlick in jungle history," confirmed the monkey solemnly.

Nugget deadpanned: "Yes, heir to the throne... based on hair. Next up: democracy by dandruff."

"Plus," Finn added, bouncing with infectious enthusiasm, "think of the stories! Future generations singing about the time you brought harmony to the jungle! Epic tales of the Feathered Queen who united predator and prey!"

Nugget flicked a stray feather back into place. "Or future generations laughing about the time the jungle put a crown on a chicken because of a bad feather day."

The dreams rushed back—those golden visions where animals bowed and ancient voices spoke her name with reverence. The feeling of destiny, of being chosen for something important.

"It would be pretty amazing," she admitted.

"Amazing?" Finn's eyes sparkled. "It would be legendary! And you deserve recognition for everything you've done. The tiger rivalry mediation, the cooperative programs, the way you naturally bring out the best in everyone..."

"I have been getting better at the leadership thing." Nugget adjusted her flower crown, as if checking whether it sat straight.

"Because it's your calling." The badger's gaze held steady. "Some animals are born to burrow, others to fly. You were born to lead."

From the edge of the clearing, a cluster of older animals watched the proceedings with varying degrees of disapproval.

The ancient tortoise shook his head, voice rasping with age. "Absolute nonsense. Seventy years in this jungle, and now they want to crown poultry based on parlor tricks."

"The storm's prediction was impressive," admitted a pragmatic porcupine. "But one lucky guess doesn't make someone royal."

"Next thing you know, they'll be consulting chickens about migration routes," snorted an elderly badger.

A practical-minded raccoon family peeked from their nearby den. "Let them play dress-up," the matriarch said dismissively. "Doesn't hurt anyone, and maybe it keeps the youngsters entertained."

"What happens when the novelty wears off?" her mate asked.

"Same thing that always happens with these enthusiasms—they move on to the next shiny thing."

Near the watering hole, a group of middle-aged animals discussed the developments with resigned amusement.

"My daughter wants to attend the 'royal coronation,'" sighed a deer. "Apparently, it's the social event of the season."

"Could be worse." The otter gave a slow shrug. "Could be another territorial war. At least this nonsense is peaceful."

The hawk's gaze darkened. "For now. Wait until someone decides they want to be emperor instead of settling for queen."

As the afternoon wore on, Nugget found herself increasingly torn between the appeal of official recognition and Kaya's practical warnings.

"The thing is," she confided to her friends during a private moment, "the dreams have been getting stronger. More detailed. Like something's trying to tell me this really is my path."

"Dreams can be influenced by daily experiences," Kaya said gently. "All this prophecy talk, the attention, the stress—that could easily create vivid dreams about destiny."

"But what if they're real?" Nugget asked. "What if I really am meant for this?"

"Then you'll prove it through your actions, not through ceremonies," Kaya replied. "True leadership doesn't need coronations to validate it."

Finn, who'd been unusually quiet during this exchange, finally spoke up.

"What if we're making this too complicated?" he said. "Nugget, you've been acting like a leader for weeks. Animals come to you with problems, you help solve them, they trust your judgment. The ceremony doesn't make you a leader—it just acknowledges what you already are."

"Plus." His eyes lit up. "It would be the most spectacular party this jungle has ever seen."

Nugget looked around at the expectant faces—animals who seemed genuinely excited about the possibility of having her as their official leader, friends who supported her despite their different perspectives, and a jungle that had somehow become more peaceful under her accidental guidance.

"Alright," she said finally. Excitement tugged at her nerves. "Let's do this properly. But if I'm going to be a queen, we're doing it my way—with input from everyone, including the skeptics."

"Even the grumpy tortoise?" Finn asked hopefully.

"Especially the grumpy tortoise. If this is going to work, it needs to work for everyone."

The delegation erupted in cheers, immediately beginning to plan what promised to be the most elaborate coronation ceremony in jungle history.

Kaya shook her head but smiled. "Just remember—ceremonies are easy. Governing is hard."

"I'll try not to let the crown go to my head," Nugget let out a cheeky grin.

Kaya's eyes roamed the clearing, noting the animals already practicing their bows. "Too late. But at least you're aware of it."

The next week transformed the jungle into a festival of organized chaos. Every community wanted to contribute something special to the coronation ceremony.

The monkeys insisted on aerial acrobatics. The beavers designed elaborate water features. The birds composed competing symphonies. Even the usually practical badgers got caught up in the excitement, engineering a sound system that could carry Nugget's voice across the entire gathering.

Kaya tracked the parrots' synchronized flight as they spelled out "LONG LIVE THE QUEEN". "This is getting ridiculous."

"Ridiculously amazing," Finn corrected, adding choreographed leaps to his honor guard routine. "When has this jungle ever had something this spectacular to celebrate?"

The skeptics continued their grumbling but found themselves drawn into the preparations despite their reservations. The ancient tortoise complained constantly about "unnecessary pageantry" while meticulously carving ceremonial stones. The practical raccoons organized supply logistics while muttering about "wasted resources on frivolity."

Even animals who thought the whole thing was silly began to look forward to the party.

The coronation ceremony itself became the first real test of Nugget's leadership style. When the flower crown kept sliding off her head, she laughed and asked the audience to help adjust it. When the ceremonial perch collapsed under the weight of too many decorations, she made jokes about "testing the furniture before making any major policy decisions."

Instead of a solemn ritual of divine appointment, it became a community celebration where everyone felt included.

Nugget spread her wings slightly. "I accept this role—not because prophecy demands it, but because whatever this new thing is, it's worth seeing through... and it might even be fun."

The cheers that followed came not just from believers in destiny, but from animals who appreciated her practical approach to mystical authority.

As the ceremony concluded and animals dispersed to continue their festival, Kaya approached Nugget's new royal perch.

"How do you feel about it?" she asked. "Being officially in charge?"

Nugget adjusted her crown—now properly secured with engineering assistance from the beavers—and considered the question.

"Terrified and excited in equal measure," she admitted. "The attention is wonderful, and I do think I can help animals work together better. But you're right about the responsibility part being harder than the fun part."

"Just remember," Kaya said, "the crown doesn't make you right about everything. It just makes you responsible for the consequences when you're wrong."

"I'll try to be wrong as little as possible," Nugget replied. "And when I am wrong, I'll try to fix it quickly."

"Also, if this all collapses, the crown doubles as a fruit bowl. Practicality is leadership, too." Nugget deadpanned.

From across the clearing, animals continued celebrating their new queen—some because they believed in prophecy, some because they appreciated effective leadership, and some because they enjoyed having something positive to celebrate.

The transition was complete. Nugget was no longer an accidental mediator but an official leader, with all the pageantry and responsibility that entailed.

Feathers and Factions

The jungle had never seen quite this level of organized chaos.

Word of Nugget's prophetic pronouncements during the games had spread like wildfire through the canopy grapevine, but not everyone was singing her praises. The shift from curious entertainment to a full-fledged political movement had created divisions.

Near the eastern groves, a family of capuchin monkeys worked frantically to hang banners made of woven leaves between the trees. "LONG LIVE THE COWLICK CROWN" swayed in the morning breeze.

"My tail's getting sore from all this flower-waving," one monkey grumbled.

"Better than getting your tail bitten off by hawks. Haven't seen a raid since we started this."

"Think she's really magic?"

"Think I really care? My kids sleep through the night now."

Near Nugget's clearing, younger animals had built a shrine from sticks and stones, bowing before a crude wooden chicken.

"Cowlicked one, feathered one—"

"Oh, stuff it." An ancient tortoise shuffled past. "Seventy years in this jungle, and now they're praying to poultry."

At the watering hole, a badger merchant loaded his cart while whistling cheerfully.

"Business is good?" asked a passing otter.

"Trade routes stay open when nobody's fighting over territory. Whatever she's doing, it's working."

"Even if she's just a lucky chicken?"

"Especially if she's just a lucky chicken. Lucky's more reliable than magic."

Across the watering hole, Bruiser the Boar stood belly-deep in mud, his tusks gleaming. With exaggerated solemnity, he bowed so low he toppled forward, splashing face-first into the water. His followers erupted in snorts.

"Your Majesty! Shall we request permission to drink? Or perhaps convene a committee on hydration protocols?"

From her hammock between the tiger territories, Nugget titled her crown of flowers. At her feet lay the usual fruits, blossoms, polished stones—but today they looked less like trinkets and more like tribute.

She grumbled to herself, "Five more minutes before I peck someone for interrupting my morning contemplation."

But the delegation already approached, larger than yesterday's, wings and paws carrying petitions instead of gossip.

A finch landed nervously on a nearby branch.

"Your Majesty... the ants are asking if their excavation needs official approval. They say it crosses into what they're calling... crown territory."

Crown territory? When had that happened?

"Tell them to use their best judgment and ask if they need help with materials or coordination."

The finch's eyes went round.

"Such wisdom! Such care for even the smallest subjects!"

It zipped off, chirping praises to anyone who would listen.

Nugget poked at her crown with a sigh. "All I said was *yes*."

Kaya and Finn's eyes met across their morning patrol positions.

"This isn't just about us anymore, is it?" Finn watched more animals gather at the edges of the clearing.

"No. It's bigger than our rivalry ever was. But what exactly is it becoming?"

High in the mahogany tree that doubled as the aviary council chamber, feathers rustled like campaign posters in the wind.

On the north side, the Believers swayed in unison, harmonizing hymns about feathered destiny and the holiness of cowlicks. A scarlet macaw named Chorus conducted with the zeal of someone auditioning for prophet-in-chief.

"The prophecy demands celebration! Our songs honor the ancient words made manifest!"

Opposite them, the Skeptics staged musical counter-programming—satirical squawks, mock coronations, and chicken struts so overblown they had ground animals rolling with laughter.

"Better honest laughter than blind worship," said their spokesman, Wit the blue jay, between wing-flaps. "Besides, the prophecy's vague enough to crown any bird with bad feathers."

From her hammock below, Nugget sighed.

"Funny. The only difference I see between the two sides is which branch they've claimed." She plucked up a peeled lychee and snapped it down. "At least the believers are in tune."

Kassandra darted back and forth like an overworked referee, feathers fluffed with frustration.

"Unity! Your hymns are alienating other species, and your mockery is dividing us further—"

Neither side listened. Believers sang louder. Skeptics flapped harder.

High above, two falcons circled with disdain.

"Three seasons of parrot leadership," one said, ruffling his feathers. "And she's reduced to breaking up choir practice."

"Meanwhile, predators like us take orders from poultry. Perhaps it's time birds of prey had their own branch."

Despite the jungle's new political tangles, Nugget was starting to see results. When word came of a five-day standoff between porcupines and wild dogs, she didn't hesitate.

"Finn, this one's yours. Kaya already tried the logical route."

Kaya winced, still favoring her injured leg.

"All I did was quote jungle law. Somehow that made everyone angrier."

"Exactly. They don't need statutes. They need a story."

When Finn arrived, the clearing was heavy with tension—porcupine quills raised, dog teeth bared, five days of resentment buzzing in the air. He burst in like a one-tiger parade.

He spun into the center, scattering flower petals with a dramatic bow.

"PERFECT! Do you know where you're standing?"

Both families froze. Suspicion. Confusion.

Finn spread his paws wide, as though unveiling a sacred stage.

"This... is the legendary Sunset Grove! The very place where the Great Peace was forged, three generations

93

past, between the Wise Porcupine Chief and the Noble Dog Alpha!"

A porcupine blinked. The dogs exchanged wary glances. None of them had heard of this, but Finn's voice rolled like scripture.

He lowered into a solemn crouch, eyes sweeping the crowd.

"They were just like you. Families to protect, pride at stake. But they realized this grove was blessed—abundant enough for all. The spirits demanded wisdom."

The dog alpha's ears twitched.

"What kind of wisdom?"

Finn's tail flicked like a conductor's baton.

"Time-sharing! Dogs by day, swift and fierce under the sun. Porcupines at dawn and dusk, cautious and clever in the twilight. No clashes, no losses. And prosperity for all!"

A pause. The porcupine matriarch's quills softened a fraction.

"That... doesn't sound impossible."

Finn leaned close, lowering his voice to a conspiratorial whisper.

"Of course, legend warns that anyone who breaks the Sunset Peace soon finds their luck... rotting."

A dramatic beat. Then a shrug. "But that's probably just a story."

The families shifted, suddenly seeing the grove differently. Golden light slanted through branches. Berries gleamed like treasure. The idea of sharing no longer seemed outrageous.

Within an hour, they had a schedule. Dogs claimed late afternoon hunts, porcupines dawn foraging. Both avoided the blazing noon. Both left convinced the grove had been waiting for this solution.

As the newly cooperative families dispersed, Kaya approached Finn with her mouth hanging open.

"What?"

"Sunset Grove? The Great Peace? Did you just... make all that up?"

Finn's theatrical mask dropped, replaced by embarrassment mixed with pride.

"Every word. But look—it worked."

"They just needed a way to back down without losing face," Kaya admitted. "They'd have agreed to almost any story that let them save dignity."

From the tree line, an elderly badger shook his head at his companion.

"Great Peace, my tail. My grandfather would have mentioned a ceremony that important. But if it gets them to shut up about territory rights..."

"Think they actually believe it?" his companion asked.

"Think it matters? They get their schedule, we get some quiet, and that showboat tiger gets to feel clever. Everyone wins."

From her perch nearby, Nugget watched with quiet satisfaction as the two tigers—once consumed by rivalry—now leaned forward eagerly, acknowledging each other's triumphs.

"That was amazing! How did you know exactly what story to tell?"

Finn's grin returned, but now it carried confidence rather than just showing off. "I've been watching audiences my whole life. Turns out, the same tricks that make them cheer... can make them cooperate."

That night, she sank into her hammock among the day's offerings and notes, the air thick with new responsibilities. The days of tiger squabbles and absurd kidnappings felt far away, replaced by disputes, alliances, and endless compromise.

Still, there was progress. Finn weaving stories into peace. Kaya bending her logic into something more flexible. Even unlikely partnerships taking root.

Far off, in the ancient grove where shadows pooled like dark water, Calypso bent over his reports by firelight. Each line recorded the chicken's growing influence, every crack in the old order. He laid the scroll aside, eyes fixed on the darkness.

Tomorrow, choices would have to be made.

Strength and Tradition

Dawn brought the confirmation Calypso had been dreading. A young ocelot scout approached his resting place, spotted coat trembling.

"Sir, the border watchers report three more communities have joined the chicken's territories."

Calypso lifted his massive head from his paws. "Voluntarily?"

"They sent delegations requesting membership. The Riverside Beavers, the Canopy Monkeys, and the Hilltop Badgers. All asking to adopt what they're calling 'cooperative governance protocols.'"

Stratos emerged from the shadows where he'd been sharpening his claws. "And their reasons?"

The scout glanced between the two apex predators uncertainly. "Trade benefits, sir. Conflict resolution. Something about 'sustainable resource management' and 'inclusive decision-making frameworks.'"

"Show me." Calypso rose to his feet with fluid grace.

An hour later, Calypso crouched in the undergrowth overlooking Riverside Territory. What he saw challenged everything he'd built his leadership on.

Beavers—natural engineers and typically territorial decision-makers—sat in a circle with rabbits, squirrels, and a family of mice. But this wasn't chaos. The discussion flowed with surprising efficiency.

"The upstream modifications will affect everyone downstream," a large beaver was explaining, "so we need input from all affected parties."

"But we don't understand dam engineering," protested a rabbit.

"You understand flooding patterns," the beaver replied, nodding. "We need both kinds of knowledge."

A squirrel traced drainage routes on a bark map while mice identified vulnerable burrow systems. Within an hour, they'd developed a comprehensive flood management plan that protected everyone's territory.

"Efficient," Stratos murmured beside him. "No disputes, no power struggles."

"For flood management," Calypso agreed reluctantly. "But watch what happens when pressure arrives."

As if summoned by his words, a messenger hawk landed with urgent news.

"Flash flood warning from the northern mountains. Massive surge expected in two hours. Multiple territories at risk."

Calypso watched twenty-three animals debate evacuation procedures while water levels rose around their feet.

"We should form an emergency response committee," suggested the beaver council leader.

"But evacuation affects everyone," a rabbit protested. "Shouldn't we vote on the routes?"

"What about consultation with burrow-dwellers who can't use tree highways?" added a mouse representative.

A beaver kit squeaked in terror as water reached the burrow entrance. Calypso's muscles coiled. Every instinct screamed at him to grab the kit, bark orders, save lives.

Instead, he watched democracy nearly drown a child.

"We need consensus before moving forward," insisted a well-meaning badger. "Everyone's safety matters equally."

Another precious ten minutes passed as they debated whether tree routes or tunnel systems would be safer for elderly animals.

"They're going to get that kit killed," Stratos said grimly.

Water was ankle-deep when Calypso made his decision.

"Evacuation protocols now," he ordered, stepping into the clearing. His voice carried the absolute authority of someone accustomed to life-and-death decisions.

"Squirrels—tree highways for mobile animals. Rabbits—tunnel routes for families with young. Mice—elderly and infirm to elevated positions immediately."

"But we haven't finished discussing—" began the mouse representative.

"No time." Calypso was already moving, scooping up the terrified beaver kit with one massive paw. "Beavers, redirect flow channels. Everyone else, move according to assigned routes. Questions after we're all breathing."

The transformation was immediate. Animals who'd been paralyzed by consensus suddenly moved with coordinated efficiency.

Within an hour, every vulnerable animal was evacuated to high ground. The modified channels successfully diverted the worst surge. Zero casualties.

"Thank you," the beaver council leader said as they watched the waters recede. "We would have lost lives without your intervention."

Calypso studied the cooperative animals—intelligent, well-meaning, completely unprepared for decisions that couldn't wait for discussion.

"Your approach works fine when there's time to howl about it. But when death comes running, someone has to bare teeth first."

That evening, Calypso's own council gathered around their traditional stone circle. Instead of the usual confident briefings, uncomfortable questions hung in the air.

"Sir, the cooperative territories are expanding rapidly. Should we be concerned?"

Calypso stared into the fire, remembering the beaver kit's terrified squeak. "They saved lives today through cooperation. Then nearly lost them the same way."

"Which proves cooperation doesn't work under pressure."

Calypso's claws scraped against stone. The sound echoed like doubt given voice.

"Does it? Or does it prove they need practice making hard choices quickly?"

An uncomfortable silence settled over the council. A log cracked in the fire, sending sparks spiraling upward.

"Sir? Are you suggesting their system might... improve?"

Calypso rose from his position, pacing to the edge of their firelight where shadows began. He turned back to face his council, but his expression carried something none of them had seen before— uncertainty.

"Today I saved lives by making decisions they couldn't make fast enough. But tomorrow? Next week? I can't be everywhere when a crisis strikes."

"Then they'll fail. And remember why strength has led for generations."

Calypso's gaze returned to the fire, watching flames consume wood with patient inevitability. "What if they don't fail? What if they learn?"

The question hung in the smoky air like an uncomfortable truth none of them wanted to examine.

As his advisors dispersed into the night, Calypso remained by the dying fire. The day's events replayed in his mind—not just the flood rescue, but the moment after. The beaver council's genuine gratitude. Their immediate discussion of how to handle similar emergencies without external intervention.

They weren't angry about his interference. They were learning from it. His father's voice echoed from memory: *The strong protect the weak. But who protects them when the strong are wrong?*

A stick snapped in the darkness. Calypso's head turned toward the sound but saw only shadows dancing in the wind. The sound reminded him of something fragile breaking under pressure.

Tonight, for the first time in his life, Calypso wondered if his father had been asking the right question all along.

The cooperative territories continued their evening routines—animals settling into shared dens, collaborative watches, the murmur of communities that had chosen to trust each other. Beautiful sounds.

Fragile sounds.

As the fire died to embers, Calypso listened to those distant voices and felt something crack inside his chest—not broken but splitting open like a seed that had been dormant too long.

From the darkness, a messenger bird's cry echoed once, then fell silent. Tomorrow would bring its own tests. Tonight, doubt was enough.

Two Together

The morning sun filtered through the canopy as Nugget perched in her hammock, adjusting the crown of flowers that had become her unofficial symbol of authority. Around her, the jungle hummed with its usual activity, but there was an undercurrent of concern that hadn't been there the day before.

"I have a job for both of you," she said as Kaya and Finn approached for their daily briefing. "And I'm confident you'll handle it together beautifully."

Kaya and Finn shared a comfortable look—not the old rivalry glance, but the easy acknowledgment of partners who had learned to work in harmony.

"What kind of job?" Kaya asked. She was already pulling out her bark notebook to coordinate with Finn.

"Six young animals have gone missing over the past few days. Their families are starting to panic."

Finn's ears perked up with concern. "Missing? Like, they wandered off, or something more serious?"

"Missing like they were here yesterday and gone today," Nugget replied. "No signs of struggle, no obvious threats. They just... vanished."

Kaya jotted notes while Finn paced, each turn sharper than the last. "How many? Which families? What's the timeline?" she asked.

"Little Pip the squirrel, Bounce the young rabbit, Chirp and Trill the twin finches, Tumble the badger kit, and Splash the young otter."

Within twenty minutes, both tigers had approached the problem exactly as they'd learned to do—as partners leaning on each other's strengths.

"Different species, different territories, but look—" Kaya pointed to carefully marked locations on her map while Finn listened attentively. "All early morning disappearances. All young but not helpless."

"And every family said the same thing," Finn added, building on her analysis. "Their kids seemed happy, secretive, like they knew something wonderful was going to happen."

"So, we need to examine the physical evidence and interview families," Kaya continued.

"While thinking like young animals about what adventure would be worth the risk," Finn finished.

Initially, their collaborative problem-solving methods felt natural. But as they began their investigation, old habits started creeping back in.

At the first missing animal's home, Kaya spread out her detailed maps while Finn began asking the parents about their child's recent behavior.

"We should start with a methodical grid search of the immediate area," Kaya suggested, pointing to her carefully marked zones.

"Actually," Finn interjected, "I think we need to focus on where young animals naturally gather. The old storytelling circle, the play areas—"

"Those aren't necessarily where they disappeared from," Kaya pointed out, a hint of her old impatience creeping in.

"But they might be where they planned whatever they're doing," Finn countered, his voice taking on a familiar competitive edge.

They caught themselves mid-argument and laughed.

"Sorry," Kaya said. "Reflex."

"Mine too," Finn agreed. "Let's do the grid search first, then check the gathering spots."

As the morning progressed, the old patterns grew stronger. The stress of worried parents and the pressure to solve the mystery quickly began undermining their partnership.

Kaya found tiny paw prints and broken twigs suggesting group movement northward, but when she tried to show Finn, he was already following his own lead toward what he suspected was a secret meeting spot.

"Finn," she called, frustration rising. "The physical evidence is pointing this way."

He didn't look up. "And the behavioral evidence is pointing that way."

"We agreed to work together."

"We are working together. Just... efficiently. I'll check my lead, you check yours."

"That's not working together, that's working separately!"

"It's covering more ground!"

"It's exactly what we used to do!"

They both stopped, staring at each other across the clearing.

"Oh," Kaya said.

"Yeah," Finn agreed, looking embarrassed. "We're doing it again, aren't we?"

"When did we start second-guessing each other again?" Kaya asked, setting down her maps with a sigh.

"Probably when we got worried about not finding them quickly enough." Finn shook his head, abandoning his artistic theories about secret gathering spots. "Old habits under pressure."

"The parents are scared. That made us scared. And when we're scared..."

"We fall back on what feels familiar," Finn finished. "Even when we know better."

Kaya looked at her organized evidence while Finn studied his behavioral insights. "You know what's ridiculous? We actually found complementary clues. Your gathering spot theory explains my group movement evidence."

"And your physical tracking gives direction to my behavioral hunches," Finn agreed. "We just started treating them like competing ideas instead of puzzle pieces."

"So, what do we know when we put it together?"

Working as true partners again, they quickly assembled the complete picture.

"Young animals have been gathering at the old storytelling circle," Finn reported, "asking questions about celebration planning and Nugget's favorite things."

"And then moving in an organized group toward the hidden grove," Kaya added, showing the trail evidence. "They've been stockpiling resources and practicing something."

"Celebration supplies and secret rehearsals," they said together.

"They're planning some kind of surprise," Kaya realized.

"But how did they get through the thorny barrier to reach the grove?" Finn wondered.

Kaya studied her maps with a fresh perspective, incorporating Finn's suggestion to think like young animals. "They didn't go through it. They went over it—using the Squirrel Highway that adults are too heavy for."

"The branch route over the thicket!" Finn exclaimed. "That's brilliant. And completely something kids would think of."

Following their combined analysis, they made their way to the hidden grove via the longer adult route, leading to the same destination their quarry had reached through ingenuity.

What they found made them both stop in amazement.

The grove was transformed into an elaborate celebration space. Flower garlands hung between trees in carefully planned patterns. A raised platform made of woven branches stood at the center, decorated with colorful petals and polished stones.

And working with the focused intensity of professional event planners were six young animals, each contributing their unique skills to create something beautiful.

"The flower arrangements need to be higher on the left side," Pip the squirrel directed. "Nugget's favorite colors are yellow and orange."

"The song needs another verse about friendship," Chirp the finch tilted his head, letting the melody linger.

"The welcome dance is almost ready," Bounce the rabbit demonstrated.

"Do you think she'll like the miniature throne?" Tumble the badger showed off the carved wooden gifts.

"The acoustics are perfect from here," Splash the otter reported.

"This is going to be the best thank-you celebration ever," little Trill supervised.

Kaya and Finn watched in silent amazement.

"They've been planning this for weeks," Kaya whispered.

"And keeping it secret from every adult in the jungle," Finn added with professional admiration. "That's impressive coordination."

"Should we let them know we found them?"

"Absolutely not. This is too perfect to interrupt."

Making their way quietly back to Nugget's clearing, they walked in comfortable partnership. Kaya found herself automatically adjusting her pace to match

Finn's, while he instinctively paused when she stopped to examine something interesting. The coordination happened without discussion, without planning—just two animals who had learned to move as a team.

Even when they occasionally forgot how.

"We're pretty good at this when we don't get in our own way." Finn grinned.

"Amazing how fear makes us revert to old patterns," Kaya agreed. "Even when we know better."

"At least we caught ourselves before we completely messed it up."

"And figured out how to get back on track."

They found Nugget waiting anxiously for news about her missing young subjects.

"Well?" she asked immediately. "Did you find them? Are they safe?"

"They're perfectly safe," Kaya reported. "And exactly where they're supposed to be."

"And they're working on something that's going to absolutely amaze you," Finn added with a grin. "But we can't tell you what because it's a surprise."

"A surprise?"

"The best kind," both tigers exchanged a glance, smirks matching perfectly.

Nugget watched them and smiled. They looked like the partnership they'd worked to become— comfortable, complementary, occasionally imperfect, but genuinely united.

"I take it you two learned something about working together under pressure?"

"We learned that we're still learning," Kaya admitted.

"And that's okay," Finn added. "As long as we keep choosing to work together instead of falling back into old habits."

"Also, your young subjects are excellent at project management and event planning."

"And keeping secrets from adults is apparently a universal skill among children of all species."

Nugget settled back with a satisfied smile. "In that case, I suppose we should pretend to be very worried about the missing animals for a few more days."

"How long should we keep up the worried act?" Kaya asked.

"Until they're ready to surprise us," Nugget replied. "Which, knowing young animals and secret projects, should be just about when they can't keep the secret anymore."

At that precise moment, distant sounds of enthusiastic but badly coordinated singing drifted through the jungle from the direction of the hidden grove.

"Two days," Finn predicted. "Maybe three."

"Two days," Kaya agreed, making a note. "I should start preparing my surprised face."

"We should both practice being surprised," Finn added. "This is going to require some acting skills."

"Again, what exactly should I be preparing to be surprised about?" Nugget asked curiously.

"That," both tigers said in unison, "would ruin the surprise."

The Feast of Unity

"EMERGENCY EXPANSION!" a capuchin monkey called out. "Apparently, everyone in the jungle wants to come to the thank-you party!"

"Well," Nugget said to the six beaming organizers, "I think your 'small thank-you celebration' got a little out of hand."

"We were," Pip chittered excitedly, adjusting a garland that had tripled in size since morning. "But then everyone wanted to come. And then their friends came. And then—"

"And now we're feeding half the jungle," Bounce finished, hopping past with an armload of freshly woven place mats.

Tables made from broad leaves stretched between the trees, groaning under platters of roasted nuts, fermented fruit, and what the monkeys insisted was "victory cake" but looked suspiciously like mud decorated with berries.

"Try the cake," Finn suggested, settling beside Nugget's coconut throne. "It's... educational."

"What's in it?"

"Better not to ask. The capuchins were very enthusiastic about the recipe."

A group of young monkeys chose that moment to launch into an impromptu food fight, sticky mangoes flying through the air and splattering guests.

Kassandra leaned back on her perch, wings crossed. "This is exactly what I expected. Chaos masquerading as leadership."

Nugget felt her stomach drop. But instead of panic, she found herself laughing.

"You know what?" she called to the monkey combatants. "If we're going to have a food fight, let's do it properly."

She grabbed an overripe banana and lobbed it with surprising accuracy at the monkey ringleader, who caught it expertly and grinned.

"Teams!" Nugget said. "Fruit-throwers versus nut-rollers. But only volunteers, and only with fruit that's already fallen."

Within minutes, what could have been a disaster became the evening's entertainment. The sloths volunteered as referees, their deliberate movements perfect for tracking projectiles.

Kassandra's beak hung open as she watched order emerge from chaos.

The parrot ruffled her feathers. "She turned a food fight into a game."

"With rules," added a nearby sparrow. "And referees. And cleanup crews."

Moments later, a territorial dispute erupted between two porcupine families over honey-glazed grubs, quills bristling as other animals backed away nervously.

Nugget hopped down from her throne and approached the agitated porcupines.

"Is there a problem here?"

"They took our grubs," one porcupine complained.

"We were here first," the other family protested.

Nugget examined the situation, then pointed her wing toward a nearby tree where larger, more succulent grubs clung to the bark.

"Those honey-glazed ones are good," she said conversationally, "but have you tried the tree-sweet variety? They're only ripe this time of the year."

Both families looked where she pointed, their dispute momentarily forgotten.

"I've never seen those before," one admitted.

"My grandmother used to harvest those," said another, "but I thought they'd gone extinct in this area."

"Not extinct. Just overlooked."

Within moments, the porcupines were working together to harvest the tree grubs, their earlier conflict forgotten.

As the food fight settled into organized chaos, animals began lining up to touch Nugget's perch.

"For luck," explained a nervous rabbit.

"Does it work?" asked another.

"Can't hurt. She did turn a storm into a victory somehow."

A family of weasels pushed forward, voices carrying across the clearing: "Always believed in cooperation! From day one! Ask anyone!"

"Weren't you calling her 'that ridiculous bird' last month?" a squirrel asked innocently.

"That was... a test of faith. We were testing our faith."

Nearby, possums clustered around Kaya with bark scrolls: "We wrote songs about her wisdom. Seventeen of them. Think she'd want to hear them all? Maybe grant us that nice hollow tree by the creek?"

Kassandra landed beside Nugget with a soft thud. "Half of them discovered their devotion after you started winning."

"The other half?"

"Still deciding if you're worth the investment."

As evening approached, a sudden commotion erupted near the food tables. A young toucan chick had fallen from its perch, landing awkwardly with a clearly injured wing.

Panic rippled through the bird section. The chick's parents swooped frantically while others squawked in distress.

Kassandra started to fly down to take charge but froze when she saw Nugget already moving.

"Everyone step back, please. Give them room to breathe." Nugget's voice cut through the chaos. She turned to the parents. "I know this is frightening, but let's focus on helping."

She quickly organized the response: soft moss for the chick to rest in, a butterfly scout to fetch the jungle's healer, and calm animals to keep predators away while maintaining respectful distance.

"Has anyone seen this type of injury before?" Nugget asked.

An old parrot stepped forward. "The wing isn't broken, just sprained. With proper care, it should heal completely."

"Thank you. Would you mind helping coordinate care until our healer arrives?"

When the ancient turtle healer confirmed the chick would recover fully, cheers went up from the gathered animals. Nugget didn't take credit—instead, she thanked everyone who'd helped.

As the feast wound down, Kassandra made a decision that surprised even herself.

She flew down and landed beside Nugget's perch.

"That was... impressive," she said.

"The prophecy fulfillment?" Nugget steadied her crown nervously.

Kassandra's laugh was sharp. "The prophecy? Please. I've seen three different 'chosen ones' in neighboring territories. Two turned tyrant, one got eaten by his own supporters. Prophecies are just political theater with better marketing."

She fixed Nugget with a calculating stare. "But the way you handled that chick, mediated the porcupine dispute, turned chaos into cooperation—that's skill. Learned skill. That's why I'm here."

"So, you don't think I'm fulfilling ancient destiny?"

"I think you're a chicken who figured out how to lead. The prophecy just gives everyone a story to feel special about. But the leadership? That's real."

Nugget's feathers ruffled with embarrassment. "I mostly just tried not to make things worse."

"Exactly. Do you know how rare that is?" Kassandra's sharp confidence softened. "I owe you an apology. I judged you before I really understood what you were trying to do. This jungle needs what you're offering."

A slow smile spread across Nugget's beak. "Does this mean...?"

"It means I'd like to help. If you'll have me."

Kaya and Finn, who'd been watching with barely concealed amazement, approached cautiously.

"So," Finn grinned. "Does this mean no more bird politics drama?"

Kassandra laughed—a surprisingly warm sound. "Oh, there will always be bird politics. But now we'll have someone with sense helping to sort it out."

As the animals dispersed, still buzzing about Nugget's "masterful" crisis response, the old turtle healer approached Clive quietly.

"That chick would have been fine regardless," the healer said. "Minor sprain. Heals in a few days with or without moss cushions and organized sympathy."

"But the parents felt better having something to do," Clive replied. "And everyone else felt better watching their leader 'solve' a problem that was already solving itself."

The healer's ancient eyes twinkled. "Funny thing—sometimes it's not the injury that needs tending, but the fear around it."

Nearby, two possums whispered:

"Did you see how she organized everyone? Such wisdom!"

"My cousin says the chick was already improving before she even showed up," the other replied. "But don't tell anyone. Apparently, that's not the inspiring version."

As the last guests departed and fireflies dimmed their lights, Nugget looked around at the transformed clearing. The evening had been chaotic, unpredictable, and occasionally alarming.

It had also been wonderful.

"You know," she said to her friends—and Kassandra was definitely included now— "I think I'm starting to understand this leadership thing."

"Just remember." Kassandra's tone cut like a claw. "Good leadership is like a good feast. It takes planning, cooperation, and the wisdom to know when to let things get a little messy."

Nugget laughed, preening her feathers as she settled in for the night. The jungle had found its rhythm, and Nugget had found her place in it.

The Crown's Burden

The morning after the feast brought visitors.

A stern badger marched into Nugget's clearing without invitation, his claws already extended. Behind him skulked a nervous-looking rabbit clutching what appeared to be a petition made of leaves.

Nugget was barely awake, still picking flower petals from her crown. "Good morning?"

The badger didn't return the greeting. Instead, he began digging furiously at the base of a nearby tree, sending dirt flying in all directions.

"What are you—" Nugget began.

"Territory markers!" The badger snarled between shovel-fulls of earth. "If prey animals are making decisions about predator territories, then predators mark new boundaries!"

"But that's my breakfast tree," protested a squirrel who'd been quietly cracking nuts in the branches above.

"Not anymore!" The badger's digging intensified. "Natural order demands clear lines!"

The rabbit hopped forward nervously. "We represent the Coalition for Equal Voices, and we demand—" He paused, squinting at his leaf notes. "We demand... um... what do we demand again?"

"Everyone gets a say in everything!" squeaked a second rabbit from behind the first.

"But you're not from this territory."

"Fair treatment knows no boundaries!" the first rabbit declared, then immediately looked confused by his own words.

The badger paused his digging to glare at them. "Fair treatment is chaos! Strength maintains order!" He resumed his furious excavation.

"Shouldn't we vote on that?" the second rabbit asked.

"Vote on what?"

"Whether strength maintains order."

"We could form a group to study voting on things," suggested a third rabbit who'd materialized from nowhere.

Meanwhile, the badger's digging had uncovered the squirrel's winter nut cache. Acorns scattered everywhere.

"Those are mine!" the squirrel chittered in outrage.

"Natural selection!" the badger huffed. "Strong diggers, superior access!"

A shadow passed overhead. A hawk swooped down, clearly intending to make a dramatic entrance—and immediately got its talon tangled in a low-hanging vine.

"Traditional hunters don't need—ow!" The hawk twisted frantically. "Someone cut me down!"

"Are you stuck?"

"I'm making a point about sky supremacy—get me down from here!"

The badger looked up from his hole, now waist-deep in excavated earth. "This is what happens when the natural order breaks down! Hawks in trees instead of sky!"

"I wasn't supposed to be IN the tree." The hawk protested, still dangling upside-down. "This was strategic positioning!"

The rabbits had formed a small circle and were debating whether they needed permission to help free the hawk, or if rescue operations fell under some kind of emergency authority that superseded their group-decision process.

Nugget watched a family of ants methodically carrying away the badger's scattered dirt, grain by grain, while he remained oblivious in his determination to dig deeper.

"Finn," she called to the trees. "Could you...?"

Finn dropped from above, executing a perfect triple somersault before landing in a dramatic crouch with both paws spread wide. He surveyed the scene—

badger digging furiously toward the center of the earth, hawk spinning slowly in a vine noose, rabbits debating the logistics of emergency response—and grinned.

"Ladies and gentlemen, I present: 'Political Theory in Practice,' featuring special guest appearances by gravity and poor planning!"

He sprang toward the hawk with an elaborate leap, then began untangling the vine with exaggerated care, pausing between each movement to check his form. "The key to strategic positioning is knowing where you're positioning yourself strategically."

"That's the worst advice I've ever heard," the hawk grumbled.

"Thank you! I've been working on my material."

The badger emerged from his hole, now so deep only his ears were visible. "Has anyone seen the surface?" his voice echoed from below.

"You passed it about ten minutes ago."

"Traditional digging methods don't account for enthusiasm," Finn noted, peering down into the depths.

By now, a small crowd had gathered to watch the spectacle. The rabbits were still debating rescue protocols while the badger's muffled complaints drifted up from underground. The hawk, finally freed, attempted to fly away with dignity but immediately crashed into another tree.

"Motion to form a group on sky safety standards!" called one of the rabbits.

"Seconded!" called another.

"We need a vote on whether we can vote on group formation!" added a third.

Nugget hopped down from her perch and approached the badger's hole. "Would you like help getting out?"

"Natural selection!" came the defiant reply from below. "Strong diggers find their own way!"

"How's that working for you?"

"Still digging!"

The sound of claws scraping against stone echoed from the depths.

Meanwhile, the ants had finished relocating the badger's excavated dirt to construct what appeared to be a small but efficiently designed fortress around their colony entrance.

"Now that's practical engineering," said a passing turtle admiringly.

The hawks made one final attempt at coordinated intimidation by perching in formation on a dead branch, which immediately snapped under their combined weight, sending all three tumbling into the badger's abandoned dirt pile.

"Traditional perching methods require structural assessment," Finn observed cheerfully.

The rabbits paused their debate to stare at the undignified heap of feathers and indignation.

"Should we vote on whether to help them?" one asked.

"We should vote on voting!" another replied.

"I vote for voting about voting!" declared a third.

Nugget looked around at the chaos—badger stuck underground still proclaiming the superiority of his methods, hawks trying to extract themselves from a dirt pile with maximum dignity and minimum success, rabbits forming groups to discuss group formation, and ants efficiently building their fortress with materials provided by everyone else's disasters.

"You know, I'm starting to understand why some animals prefer simple solutions," she said to Kaya, who'd arrived to witness the spectacle.

"Like what?"

"Like admitting when you're stuck and asking for help."

A muffled voice drifted up from the hole: "Never!"

The badger's digging resumed with renewed determination, now accompanied by the sound of claws against solid bedrock.

"How deep does he plan to go?" a bewildered possum asked.

"Until he finds the natural order, apparently."

From above, the newly freed hawk called down: "At least I'm not underground!"

He then flew directly into the same tree for the third time.

As the various delegations eventually departed—the badger still digging, the rabbits still debating, the hawks still attempting to achieve basic flight competency—Nugget settled back onto her perch.

"That was either the most educational morning we've had in months, or the most entertaining disaster," Finn announced.

"Why not both?" Kaya suggested, making notes in her bark journal about installing warning signs around low-hanging branches.

In the distance, they could hear the badger's muffled voice: "Found water! This must be progress!"

"Should someone tell him that's probably just the underground stream?" Kaya asked.

"He'll figure it out eventually."

The sound of splashing echoed from below, followed by creative badger profanity.

"Or not," she added.

That evening, after they'd finally convinced the badger to accept a rope ladder and the hawks had agreed to practice flying in an area with fewer trees, Nugget reflected on the day's events.

"You know what I learned today?"

"That theory gets complicated when gravity gets involved?" Finn suggested.

"That groups can debate anything, including their own existence?" Kaya added.

"That everyone's an expert until they have to actually do something."

From somewhere in the distance, they heard the sound of renewed digging.

"He's at it again," Kaya observed.

"Different hole this time," Finn noted. "Progress!"

Nugget straightened her crown and settled in for the night. The badger would keep digging, the rabbits would keep debating, and the hawks would keep crashing into trees. Then a harsh call echoed from the distance.

Clearly, not everyone found incompetence quite so amusing.

Clive's ears pricked. He paused at the grove's edge, one paw moving toward his satchel.

"Was that...?" Nugget began.

"Probably nothing," Clive leaned forward slightly, eyes narrowing. "But whoever sent today's amateurs is likely getting reports about their limited success."

Another harsh call answered the first.

The crown felt heavier now, as if every petal knew what was coming.

Silver Tongue from Goldleaf

The Goldleaf Territory was the jewel of the eastern jungle. Everyone who lived there was constantly reminded of this fact by their beloved leader, Raizo the tiger. It was also notably the only territory in the region completely free of chickens, which Raizo considered one of his greatest administrative achievements.

Raizo stretched languidly on his favorite lounging rock, admiring how the morning light caught every stripe on his magnificent coat. He'd spent an hour grooming himself to perfection, and it showed.

"Magnificent morning!" he boomed to his gathered supporters.

"Oh yes, sir!" Flatter the mongoose nodded so enthusiastically that his whole body bobbed. "And you look particularly commanding today. That stripe pattern is... is it getting more symmetrical?"

Raizo's chest swelled with pleasure. "Good eye, Flatter. I've been working on my posture. Proper bearing enhances natural markings."

Chitter, the secretary squirrel, shuffled through bark papers nearby, her whiskers twitching as she organized the morning reports.

"Speaking of natural superiority," Raizo continued, his voice carrying across the perfectly manicured clearing, "I was reviewing our incredible improvements. Most dignified water system in the jungle, cleanest territory boundaries, and—" He paused dramatically. "—not a single chicken in sight."

"How do you do it, sir?" asked Swoon, a young panther whose adoration was so obvious it made other animals uncomfortable.

"Standards." Raizo swelled with pride. "Maintain proper standards, and inferior elements naturally avoid your territory. It's really quite elegant."

Count the crow shifted on his branch, feathers ruffling. "What about the chicken causing all the fuss in the central territories? The one with the cooperation experiment?"

Raizo's tail flicked sharply. "Oh, that. Completely unnatural situation. Like watching parade decorations try to run the parade."

"Some animals seem to think it's working," Count ventured.

Raizo laughed—a rich, confident sound. "Count, please. Just because something appears to function doesn't mean it's optimal. A broken water wheel might still splash, but you wouldn't call it successful engineering."

Slink the ferret approached with nervous steps, clutching reports. "Sir? Updates from the reconnaissance missions."

Raizo's eyes lit up with anticipation. "Excellent, Slink. Tell me about the chaos in central territories. I assume the amateur leadership is cracking under pressure?"

Slink consulted his notes reluctantly. "The delegations were... not entirely successful."

"Not successful how?" Raizo's tone remained cheerful, but his tail stopped swishing.

"Well, the intimidation specialist became entangled in local vegetation during his aerial superiority demonstration."

Flatter blinked. "He got stuck in a tree?"

"Multiple trees, actually. Also, the backup specialist had to read talking points from his paw, which the targets found... amusing."

Raizo's eye twitched slightly. "Amusing? Sophisticated psychological tactics amused them?"

"Sir, they laughed. Out loud. One called it 'poorly performed tragedy.'"

"And the infiltration team?" Raizo's voice remained steady, but he'd started grooming his left paw with aggressive precision.

"They confused themselves debating voting procedures and forgot their original protest."

"The diplomatic mission?"

"They saw right through it. Asked for clarification about 'voluntary cooperation frameworks' and 'non-participation consequences.' Used air quotes."

Greywhisker, an elderly badger who'd served Raizo's family for years, cleared his throat. "Sir, perhaps they're not as amateur as we assumed?"

Raizo stopped grooming abruptly. "Greywhisker, that's impossible. These were carefully planned operations using proven psychological principles."

He leaped down from his rock and began pacing, his beautiful coat rippling in the sunlight. "The problem isn't our approach. The problem is that these animals have been so damaged by amateur leadership that they've developed... defenses."

"Defenses?" Swoon asked breathlessly.

"Against competence!" Raizo's voice rose with excitement at the discovery. "Think about it—they've been eating bitter roots for so long that when someone offers them sweet fruit, they assume it's poisoned!"

Chitter looked up from her papers. "You mean they're suspicious of manipulation because they've been manipulated before?"

"I mean, they're suspicious of excellence because they've never experienced it!" Raizo corrected, warming to his theory. "This chicken—whatever her name is—has conditioned them to expect mediocrity. When they encounter true sophistication, they literally don't recognize it."

Count tilted his head. "But sir, if they can't recognize sophistication, how do we know they're wrong instead of us being—"

"Count." Raizo's voice carried gentle reproach. "Are you suggesting that a chicken—a *chicken*—might possess leadership qualities superior to those of a magnificent predator who has transformed his territory into the jungle's crown jewel?"

Count's beak opened, then closed. The question hung in the air like morning mist.

"The most insulting part," Raizo continued, resuming his pacing with renewed energy, "is that they

147

probably think their little cooperation experiment is actually working."

"The reports do suggest some success," Slink ventured quietly.

Raizo stopped mid-stride. "Success? Slink, my friend, you're confusing activity with achievement. Just because something appears busy doesn't mean it's productive. I could teach a troupe of monkeys to bang coconuts together, but that wouldn't make them musicians."

He settled back onto his rock with fluid grace, his confidence fully restored. "No, what we're witnessing is a classic case of the Emperor's New Clothes. Everyone's so invested in pretending this cooperation nonsense works that they're afraid to admit the obvious."

"Which is?" Flatter asked eagerly.

"That it's grotesque. A *chicken* giving orders to her betters? It's like watching the help redecorate your den while you're away—disgusting and unnatural." Raizo's whiskers twitched with genuine revulsion. "Every day it continues is an insult to proper order.

Not because it won't work, but because it shouldn't exist in the first place."

His lip curled with genuine disgust. "Some things are simply offensive to witness. This is one of them."

Raizo's smile turned warm and certain. "We simply need to be patient. Superior leadership doesn't chase recognition—it waits for recognition to come seeking it."

"So, we do nothing?" Greywhisker asked.

"We wait. We observe." Raizo began grooming his other paw. "When their system collapses—as it must—they'll come looking for real leadership. And who better to provide it than someone who saw the problems from the beginning?"

As his supporters began to disperse, Raizo called after them with generous magnanimity. "Remember, when they send delegations begging for proper governance—and they will—we receive them with dignity. No gloating. Superior animals don't need to say, 'I told you so.'"

"And if they don't come begging?" Greywhisker asked quietly.

Raizo's laugh was genuine and relaxed. "Oh, Greywhisker. They will. It's simply inevitable. Inferior systems always collapse eventually. And when they do, truly superior leaders are always vindicated."

In the distance, a messenger bird flew toward the central territories. Raizo watched it go, idly admiring his reflection in a nearby puddle.

A chicken. Getting recognition that belonged to someone so obviously better qualified. It wasn't personal, of course—he didn't particularly want to rule those ungrateful animals anyway.

But the principle of the thing rankled. When excellence went unrecognized, the entire natural order suffered.

Something would need to be done about that. Eventually.

For now, though, the afternoon sun felt warm on his magnificent coat, and his territory remained perfectly, blissfully chicken-free.

Cracks in the Foundation

A young hawk landed in the clearing, her talons scraping against the branch.

"Your Majesty, I bring word from the Border Territories Council."

Nugget looked up from her breakfast berries. "I thought they stayed out of everyone's business."

"They do." The hawk's feathers ruffled. "But they've had visitors—two groups asking about your leadership, military strength, and expansion plans."

Nugget felt her crest flatten. "Expansion plans? We don't have expansion plans."

"That's what they told the visitors. But the questioners seemed skeptical about 'inevitable territorial ambitions' and 'natural progression of cooperative movements.'"

Kaya padded into the clearing; her stripes still damp from the morning mist. "Did someone mention visitors asking about territorial ambitions? Because I just caught a mongoose 'surveying wildlife patterns' near our water sources."

"Another mongoose?" Nugget's suspicion sharpened.

"Different one. Excellent credentials, perfectly reasonable explanations. Too perfect."

The hawk shifted from talon to talon. "The Border Council wants to meet tomorrow at Neutral Grove. They emphasized urgency."

As the messenger departed, Nugget stared at the formal scroll. Three months ago, her biggest worry was tiger rivalry. Now, neutral territories were calling emergency meetings.

"We need to talk to Clive," she said.

Nugget didn't wait for a council debate. Some questions couldn't survive committee discussions—

they needed answers from someone who understood the shadows behind polite threats.

She hopped down from her perch and headed toward the border territories, following the faint scent of woodsmoke that always seemed to trail in Clive's wake.

The scent of smoke led her deeper into unfamiliar territory. Squirrels scattered at the sight of her. Above, branches rustled with silent watchers reporting her progress.

The hollow beneath an ancient banyan reeked of secrets. Maps plastered the walls. Scrolls, marked with careful symbols, filled organized stacks. Small stones arranged in patterns traced networks she didn't understand.

Clive sat in the center, his monocle forgotten on the floor. He stared at a single map as if it had bitten him.

"I wondered when you'd come looking." He didn't turn his head.

"After this morning's reports, I need better information. And you seem to know things others don't."

Clive finally faced her. His usual smooth confidence had cracks. "You won't like what I have to tell you."

"Try me."

He gestured at the documents—not scholarly records, but surveillance logs, behavioral charts, and territorial codes.

"This isn't the burrow of someone who helps. This is the archive of someone who uses."

Nugget's feathers prickled. "Uses how?"

"I was an information broker. I sold intelligence to whoever paid best—territory disputes, food shortages, alliance fractures, personal weaknesses."

The hollow felt smaller suddenly. "You were spying on us."

"Worse. Spies have sides. I sold to anyone with resources. And I didn't just watch conflicts—I fed them. Gave ambitious animals exactly what they needed to exploit rivals' weaknesses."

"You've been watching us for months."

"For months. Kaya and Finn's rivalry, your patterns, your fears. I even drafted a report titled 'Unstable Power Structures: Chicken in a Predator Role.'"

Nugget's claws dug into the earthen floor. "Who were you selling us to?"

"Anyone who'd pay. Predator chiefs, council spies—leaders hungry for leverage. But... that was before this morning." He hesitated, whiskers twitching. "My old reports about a 'chicken leadership experiment' made you a target when the visitors showed up. I didn't cause today's problems—but I set the stage."

A memory pricked her—the injured chick during her feast, that delicate moment when triumph could have turned to disaster. "Was that—"

"I may have provided information that made an accident likely. By the time they asked for updates, I'd decided to stop. Watching you that day... I couldn't turn it into intelligence."

Nugget moved to the burrow's edge, staring out at a jungle that suddenly felt rigged. "Why tell me now?"

"Because at first, I thought you were just another prophecy experiment. Unlikely to succeed, but lucrative to document and sell. 'Chicken tries leadership, predictably fails, buyers get intelligence about power vacuum.' Easy profit."

Clive's paws moved restlessly over his maps. "But then I watched you with those tigers. Turn their rivalry into a partnership. The feast—chaos into celebration."

His whiskers twitched. "Could have let it all collapse. Didn't."

He looked up from the scrolls, meeting her gaze directly. "That's when I realized this wasn't another doomed experiment. You weren't faking it—you were figuring it out."

His paw tapped against a map edge. "And they weren't following some ancient story. They were following you. That makes you precious... and dangerous in the eyes of everyone who profits from chaos."

Nugget's feathers shifted uncomfortably. "But why now? What we're building didn't start today."

Clive stopped pacing, his whiskers tightening. "And because those visitors? They weren't random inquiries. Someone is pulling strings—the same strings I used to pull. If you're going to survive what's coming, you need to know exactly what I was."

He raked a paw across the maps. "Every major conflict for the past decade has my scent somewhere. I told myself I was observing nature. But I was manufacturing chaos—and selling it."

"I should banish you."

"You should."

"But Kaya and Finn taught me something: animals can change. The question is—are you changing, or is this another play?"

Clive began stripping maps from the walls, stacking scrolls like evidence. "This is everything. Every shadow I helped cast. If you're going to lead, you need to understand all of it."

"We need to understand it. If you're serious about making amends, you help dismantle what you built."

Hope flickered in Clive's eyes. "You'd trust me?"

Trust seemed like the wrong word. Every instinct screamed betrayal. But survival wasn't about instincts anymore—it was about strategy. And strategy meant using every tool, even broken ones.

"I'd trust you to fix what you broke. Trust is earned. You've got earning to do. But the jungle needs healing—and you know where the wounds are."

She extended a wing. "Clive Whiskersnoot, Former Shadow Operator, Current... what exactly are you now?"

He touched her wing with his paw. "Advisor with a serious debt to repay?"

"That works. Now show me these external threats."

As Clive spread maps that reached far beyond their borders, Nugget felt the weight of something larger than leadership. She wasn't just keeping peace among friends anymore. She was preparing for a war of whispers—one fought with secrets, alliances, and predators who had no patience for her experiments.

The golden feathers in her crown caught the dim light filtering through the burrow entrance. Where were they coming from? She'd found another one clutched in her claw this morning—the fourth one this week.

"Clive," she said, still turning the feather over in her wing. "These golden feathers I keep finding—"

"Probably molted from some exotic bird that roosts above your hammock," he said without looking up from his maps. "The real mystery is why half the jungle thinks they're mystical."

Nugget blinked. "You don't think they're... special?"

"I think desperate animals will find meaning in anything that gives them hope. A golden feather, a cowlick, a chicken who accidentally proves cooperation works—it's all the same impulse. They need symbols more than they need facts."

"So, the prophecy stuff is just—"

"Theater. Useful theater, but theater." Clive adjusted his monocle, finally meeting her gaze. "The question is: do you earn the authority animals give you because of this prophecy nonsense?"

Nugget considered this. "Every day, I try to."

"Then that's what matters. Not ancient predictions, not mystical validation—just whether you're actually helping or playing dress-up in other people's faith."

Outside the burrow, evening sounds filled the jungle—monkeys chattering, birds settling into roosts, the distant splash of otters playing in the stream. Normal sounds. Peaceful sounds. The kind of sounds that made you forget enemies might be watching from the shadows.

But now Nugget knew better. Peace was fragile. And someone out there was already planning to break it.

The Price of Knowledge

Dawn broke over the jungle, but Nugget remained in her hammock, turning a golden feather over and over in her claws. She'd found it clutched in her grip when she woke—the fourth one this week. Where were they coming from?

Kaya padded into the clearing. "You're up early."

"Just thinking."

Finn appeared, turning his morning stretch into a performance. "Thinking at dawn? That sounds suspiciously like responsibility."

Nugget managed a weak smile. "Nothing's wrong."

But when a nervous finch approached with a question about storage protocols, Nugget found herself studying the bird's expression, searching for

161

hidden meanings. Was this innocent planning or intelligence gathering?

"Tell them to proceed with their best judgment."

The finch drooped, clearly wishing for firmer direction, before winging off.

"That was... unusually vague," Kaya noted.

"I trust their judgment. Not that I know any better."

Clive appeared at the edge of the clearing; his usual smooth confidence cracked like old bark.

"How are you handling it?" he asked Nugget.

"Handling what?"

"The weight. Knowing how much you don't know."

Nugget's crest flattened. "Is this part of your redemption? Teaching me paranoia?"

"Redemption for what?" Finn tilted his head.

"It's part of keeping you alive. And keeping your friends safe." Clive produced a new scroll. "This morning's intelligence: increased activity along the eastern border. Three species moving in coordinated patterns."

"Migration or expansion?"

"Exactly. The difference determines whether we prepare for refugees or war."

After Clive left to investigate the border reports, Nugget turned to her friends.

"There's something you both need to know about our intelligence advisor."

She explained everything—Clive's confession about his spy network, his role in manipulating past conflicts, his decision to come clean, and the information he'd provided about external threats.

Kaya's tail went rigid. "He was selling intelligence about us? About our rivalry?"

"For months. He says he stopped, but..."

"But once a spy, always a spy?" Finn's usual playfulness was gone. "How do we know this isn't just another layer of manipulation?"

"We don't. That's what makes this so difficult."

Kaya paced, her analytical mind working. "His information has been accurate. The external pressures, the border activity—everything he reported has checked out."

"Which could mean he's genuinely helping, or that he's orchestrating events to make himself indispensable."

"Exactly. And I can't tell which."

As the morning wore on, other animals continued their usual requests for guidance. A family of badgers approached, requesting mediation in a boundary dispute. Yesterday, this would have been a straightforward problem-solving. Today, Nugget caught herself analyzing their expressions, weighing their words for double meanings.

She leaned closer. "Tell me more about the specific boundaries."

The badgers tilted their heads in confusion at her sudden formality.

Later, a cheerful otter bounded up with news about successful fish runs in the eastern streams.

"Wonderful catches this season, Your Majesty! Enough to share with neighboring territories if you'd like."

Nugget's eyes narrowed. "Which neighboring territories?"

"Well, any that might need—"

"Who suggested sharing? Did someone ask you to mention specific territories?"

The otter's whiskers drooped. "No one suggested anything. I just thought... sharing is what we do now."

After the otter left, clearly bewildered, Nugget slumped on her perch.

"This is exhausting." She confided to her friends during their evening strategy session. "Every conversation feels like a chess match."

"You're doing it. Analyzing everyone like they might be spies. Don't let knowledge of shadows make you forget about sunlight."

"But how do I know which is which?"

"You don't." Clive padded back from the border, eyes sharp. "That's the burden of leadership at this level. You trust carefully. You verify information through multiple sources. And you remember that paranoia is a tool, not a lifestyle."

Finn's eyes narrowed. "Easy words from someone who built his career on betraying trust."

"Fair point. Which is why you should verify everything I tell you through other sources. Good intelligence work assumes some sources are compromised—even your own advisors."

"There has to be a middle path. Between naive trust and paralyzing suspicion."

"There is." Kaya offered. "You build systems that assume some bad actors while still allowing good faith cooperation."

"And you trust your instincts about people, while staying open to the possibility that anyone can surprise you—for better or worse," Clive added quietly.

As night fell, Nugget sat in her hammock adjusting her crown. Not the comfortable flower decoration, but the weight of true responsibility.

Kaya and Finn settled nearby, the day's tensions still lingering between them.

"There's something else you both need to know. About this whole 'chosen one' situation."

She gestured at her crown with one wing. "I know you've been watching me find golden feathers, speak prophetic words, all that mystical nonsense. And I know half the jungle thinks I'm some kind of divine appointment."

"And?" Kaya prompted.

"And it's ridiculous. I'm a chicken who fell into a leadership role because two tigers couldn't agree on custody arrangements. The prophecy stuff just gave everyone a story to justify following someone completely unqualified."

"But the golden feathers—" Finn tilted his head.

"Are probably shed from some exotic bird that roosts above my hammock. The prophetic words? Stress makes me babble, and sometimes stressed babbling sounds profound." She nudged her crown with visible discomfort. "The real question is: do I earn the authority animals give me because of this prophecy nonsense?"

"Every day," Kaya said firmly.

"Then that's what matters. Not ancient predictions, not mystical validation—just whether I'm actually helping or just playing dress-up in other people's faith."

The comfortable days of accidental leadership were over. The education in intentional governance had begun.

The Shadow Campaign

Intelligence reached Calypso through his usual network of scouts and informants, many recruited through channels Clive had once established.

"The mongoose confessed," his coordinator reported, ears flattened against his skull. "Everything. His network, manipulation operations, and role in destabilizing regimes. He told the chicken all of it."

The great jaguar's eyes narrowed. "Her response?"

"She kept him. Made him a trusted advisor." The panther's voice cracked slightly. "A reformed spy with complete network knowledge now serves cooperation."

Heavy silence filled the stone chamber.

"More news," the panther continued. "Sources suggest this wasn't coerced. The mongoose confessed voluntarily because of some... moral awakening."

Before Calypso could respond, footsteps echoed from the chamber entrance. Raizo emerged from the shadows, his orange coat gleaming in the firelight.

"Fascinating developments," Raizo remarked, settling uninvited onto a stone outcropping. "A spy chooses honesty. A manipulator embraces transparency. Almost inspirational."

"This is a private briefing, Raizo."

"But this affects all of us. If creatures can transform their nature through will, what does that say about rightful order?"

Raizo began pacing, his movements fluid and confident. "If a mongoose can become trustworthy through force of will, perhaps a chicken really can lead. Perhaps prey animals are qualified to make predator decisions. Perhaps everything we've believed is just... tradition."

"What's your point?" Calypso asked, though Raizo's tone made him uneasy.

"You're debating philosophy while they dismantle everything your family built... You're facing something more dangerous than opposition. This experiment makes your worldview obsolete."

He gestured toward the intelligence reports scattered across the stone table. "If the mongoose's transformation is real, cooperation isn't an idealistic experiment. It's a system that reforms the unreformable. That makes it an existential threat."

Calypso's jaw tightened. Raizo was giving voice to thoughts he'd barely allowed himself to think.

"Of course," Raizo continued with apparent casualness, "there's another interpretation."

"Which is?"

"That this 'transformation' is the most sophisticated manipulation ever seen. What better infiltration method than convincing opponents you've completely changed nature?"

Stratos leaned forward from his position near the wall. "You think the mongoose is still playing games?"

171

"A master manipulator would know exactly how to fake moral awakening. Especially if his target was an idealistic chicken wanting to believe in redemption."

"And if you're wrong? If people can really change?" Calypso asked.

"Then we're watching the birth of new power. One that doesn't just defeat opposition—it converts it. How do you fight an enemy that turns allies against you by convincing them they can become better?"

Raizo's pacing grew more agitated, his voice rising. "You're debating philosophy while they dismantle everything your family built. Every day you hesitate, more communities adopt their system. More animals believe hierarchy is optional."

"What would you suggest?" Calypso found himself asking.

"Action. Not eventually, not when convenient, but now. Before their transformation philosophy spreads so far that animals forget why strength matters."

He fixed Calypso with an intense stare. "The mongoose's confession isn't just intelligence—it's a recruitment tool. They'll prove anyone can change, and everyone deserves redemption. How many of your supporters will that appeal to?"

Sensing an opening, Raizo pressed harder, his voice dropping to a more intimate register.

"Unless you're beginning to believe it yourself. Perhaps great Calypso wonders whether he too, could 'transform' into something more... cooperative?"

Calypso's eyes flashed, but Raizo continued relentlessly.

"If a spy can become trustworthy, maybe traditional leaders can become collaborative? Maybe strength can serve instead of rule? Maybe natural order is just a choice we've been making?"

The words hit their target. Calypso's barely acknowledged doubts were being dragged into the light and mocked.

"That's enough," Calypso growled, though his voice lacked conviction.

"Is it? Because it looks like you're paralyzed by the possibility that they might be right. That maybe cooperation really is better than hierarchy."

In the following silence, Raizo's expression shifted from mockery to understanding.

"I understand the doubt. It's seductive—the idea we could all choose to be better. That complex problems have simple solutions through discussion."

He moved closer, his voice taking on an intimate tone. "But we both know what happens when idealism meets reality. When cooperation faces a crisis that can't be solved through consensus. When leaders must make choices, pleasing no one but saving everyone."

Calypso found himself nodding despite his reservations.

"The mongoose's transformation isn't proof that change is possible," Raizo continued with his voice gaining strength with every response. "It's proof they're more dangerous than we thought. They're building a religion. And religions don't debate—they convert or destroy."

"So, what do you propose?" Calypso asked, the pull of inevitability heavy in his tone.

"We test their faith. Create a crisis that cooperation cannot solve through discussion. Force them to choose between ideals and survival. When their system collapses—as it must—animals will remember why strength has ruled for generations."

Stratos nodded slowly. "Direct challenge to fundamental assumptions."

"Exactly. Not to destroy out of spite, but to prove a necessary truth. Some problems require decisive leadership that cooperation cannot provide."

Calypso felt the weight of the decision settling. Raizo's logic was compelling, even if his motivations were suspect. The alternative—accepting his worldview might be wrong—was too disturbing to contemplate.

"Very well. But this tests systems, not a conquest war. If cooperation survives a real crisis, we accept results."

"Of course," Raizo agreed, satisfaction gleaming in his eyes. "Truth doesn't need imposition—it reveals itself under pressure."

As plans took shape in the stone chamber, the two predators worked through the night. Calypso sketched tactical approaches on stone tablets while Raizo suggested psychological pressure points. Neither fully understood what the other hoped to gain, but both believed they were working toward inevitable victory.

In the distance, animals in cooperative territories continued their daily lives, unaware that forces beyond their borders were preparing to test everything they'd built together.

The shadow campaign had begun.

The Boar's Gambit

The jungle's emergency alert system—monkey calls and bird signals—erupted at dawn. A landslide had blocked the main water source, and desperate animals were already fighting over the last puddles.

Kaya arrived with her bark folder of contingency plans, water maps, and three evacuation routes. None of it mattered.

The landslide dwarfed "Major Obstruction Protocol #7." Her backup water source was choked with mud. The carefully charted escape routes now led into thorn thickets that hadn't existed last month.

Around her, chaos spread—baby monkeys wailing, old tortoises panicking, neighbors squabbling over puddles. Kaya felt her grip slip.

"Plan B!" she shouted. But Plan B needed rocks half the size.

"Plan C!" But Plan C depended on clear skies, and thunder was already rolling.

Bruiser saw his moment.

"Perfect," he grunted to his followers. "Let's watch the chicken and her planner drown in their own paperwork."

The scarred boar stomped into the clearing, flinging mud.

"Look around!" he bellowed. "Panic, puddles, useless notes. This is what your 'cooperation' delivers."

He slashed a tusk toward the landslide.

"You think rocks care about committees? You think storms read your protocols? The jungle respects one thing: power. Raw, undeniable power. While you scribble, animals die of thirst. While you hesitate, I move mountains."

Gasps rippled through the crowd. Animals nodded. Bruiser's voice thundered.

"Strength doesn't ask permission—it acts!"

From her perch, Nugget tilted her head.

"And sometimes strength waits for the meeting to finish. Otherwise, you just end up with very strong mistakes."

She flapped down beside Kaya.

"Fine. We'll take your challenge, Bruiser. But let's do it right. Three tests instead of one."

Bruiser snorted. "Strength speaks louder than your fancy words."

"Afraid?" Nugget asked sweetly. "Maybe strength isn't the only thing that matters in a crisis."

Bruiser bristled. "Fine! But when you fail, don't come squealing to me."

"Three it is," Nugget grinned. "Fair warning—I fight dirty. I use my brain."

A few animals chuckled. Even in crisis, Nugget couldn't resist showmanship.

Bruiser plunged his hooves into the earth, flinging mud everywhere. Nugget cocked her head and listened.

"Old Shell-Back," she called, "where did the water run before the landslide?"

The ancient tortoise beamed.

"There was a spring near the greenest grove. Older than my grandmother's shell."

"Exactly." Nugget turned skyward. "Keen-Eye, what do you see from your penthouse view?"

The hawk swooped.

"Two streams meeting behind the rocks. And Bruiser looks like an angry, muddy pincushion."

Snickers rippled through the crowd. In minutes, they'd located three water sources—without digging.

Bruiser, mud dripping from his snout, stared.

"How did you—?"

"Trade secret," Nugget winked. "It's called asking nicely."

Moving Mountains

Bruiser strained at boulders, grunting and swearing. Nugget asked Kaya instead.

"How do we organize this?"

Kaya snapped back into command.

"Smaller rocks first, then leverage. Chain formation. And someone tell Bruiser that intimidation doesn't work on granite."

Nugget grinned.

"Finn, make this inspiring."

Finn puffed his chest.

"Every pebble is progress! This isn't rock removal—it's performance art!"

Monkeys scrambled into position with ropes.

"Second-best climbers!" Nugget called.

"Second-best?" one yelped.

"I'm first, obviously. Keep up."

Badgers tunneled channels, delighted to be useful *and* mysterious.

By the hour's end, Nugget's crew had cleared twice Bruiser's haul—and with more laughter. Bruiser slumped beside his tiny pile.

"Impossible. You're making it look… fun."

"Everything's more fun when you're not alone," Nugget chirped. "Even moving rocks."

The Storm Arrives

Rain lashed down, turning the landslide into a waterfall. Nugget flapped into the downpour.

"Challenge three! Let's see who can keep going when the jungle rewrites the rules. Brave the storm and solve the crisis!"

A squirrel whispered, wide-eyed, "She's enjoying this."

An old badger marveled, "In my day, leaders ran from storms. This one throws parties in them."

Bruiser charged the weather like it was prey.

"Take that, cloud!"

"Bruiser," Nugget called, "the storm doesn't care."

She turned to Kaya.

"Forget the folder. What do you see *right now?*"

Kaya hesitated—then her eyes cleared.

"The rain's washing debris away. Softening the ground. We don't fight it—we work with it."

"Exactly!" Nugget cried. "Diggers, tunnel under! Monkeys, bucket brigade! Birds, lightning patrol—try not to fry, it kills the mood."

No rigid plan. No brute force. Just adaptation and absurd optimism.

Bruiser stopped, panting, watching the impossible unfold. He shook his head. "You're insane. And somehow... It's working."

"Insanity's just creativity with commitment," Nugget replied. "And we're already soaked—might as well enjoy it."

The storm raged. Kaya adapted on the fly. Finn turned labor into theater. Nugget kept panic from boiling over. And Bruiser—once he stopped fighting the sky—became the muscle that made ideas work.

By dawn, the spring was flowing. The jungle was muddy but alive.

Nugget nodded to Kaya, whose bark folder now floated as a frog's throne.

"Impressive leadership. Also, your notes have been promoted to a lily pad."

Kaya smirked.

"Sometimes the best plan is knowing when to toss the plan. Even if it feeds frogs."

The frog croaked solemnly.

Bruiser lumbered over, unsettled but sincere.

"I thought strength meant standing alone. You showed me it's about making others strong. The prophecy? Still nonsense. Half the jungle has cowlicks if you ruffle hard enough."

Nugget tilted her head.

"So, no destiny?"

"Results," Bruiser said. "You saved this place. That's leadership. Also... yelling at storms doesn't work."

He squared his shoulders.

"My herd stands with you. Not because you beat me—because you showed me strength worth following. Even if it involves mud baths and whooping badgers."

"Very enthusiastic badgers," Nugget agreed.

Bruiser blinked, tail flicking. "Didn't know badgers could whoop."

"Kaya, was that in your plan?" Finn teased.

Word of the storm victory spread—some called it prophecy, others luck, others plain hard work. Few cared which. It felt like progress.

Later, Nugget sat with Kaya.

"What if it really was just luck?" she asked.

Kaya shook her head.

"Luck mattered. But so did you. You kept us steady. That's why the luck worked."

From the shadows, not all ears were friendly. In his den, Calypso traced scars into the stone floor as he listened to reports. Cooperation spreading. Prophecy whispers. Merchants, prey, shrine-builders—all finding reasons to follow.

The jaguar's claws scraped the rock.

"If their system is strong, it survives resistance. If not... the jungle learns the truth. Tomorrow, they meet opposition.

The Lines are Drawn

The jungle held its breath. No birds sang their dawn chorus. Even the perpetually chattering monkeys had fallen silent, their instincts warning them that something was coming.

Nugget pecked at her wilting crown. Below, a squirrel scurried between makeshift barricades, tail twitching at shadows that hadn't been there yesterday.

"They're coming." Kaya's paws gripped the bark tablet, edges pressing into her fur.

A twig snapped. Every animal froze.

"False alarm!" a lookout called. "Just a branch."

No one relaxed.

Finn struck a dramatic pose, stumbled, and caught himself on a tree. "I keep rehearsing what to say if..." He trailed off, ears twitching.

"Finn," Nugget warned.

"What? Thoroughness is a virtue."

Clive appeared from behind a boulder. "Large formations moving through the deep territories. They've stopped trying to hide."

The tree line shivered. Not with wind.

Calypso stepped into the clearing. No roars, no theatrics—just a massive jaguar who looked resigned and certain. His followers lingered at the forest edge, close enough to menace, far enough to feign restraint.

Nugget hopped down. Kaya limped to her left. Finn bounded to her right. No words exchanged, no hesitation.

Calypso's amber eyes swept the scene—hawks beside rabbits, squirrels beside tortoises, predators and prey holding ground together. And at the center: a chicken.

"Nugget of the Cowlick Crown," he said formally. "I come under parley."

Nugget's head tilted with interest, already responding. "I'm listening."

"You've built something unusual," Calypso admitted. "Animals working together by choice, not fear." His gaze flicked to a rabbit taking orders from a hawk. "But it cannot last. A real crisis will tear this apart. Drought. Invasion. Plague. Consensus becomes chaos. Equality becomes weakness. Compassion kills."

He gestured toward his waiting forces. "Strength must lead. Return to order and prevent suffering."

"And if I refuse?" Nugget asked.

"Then I prove why strength has ruled for generations. Not from cruelty. From necessity."

Nugget studied him—dangerous because he truly believed it. When she spoke, her voice carried not borrowed authority but earned weight.

"You think strength means shouldering what others can't. But real strength isn't making hard choices alone. It's making them together." She pointed to the alliance around her. "Decisions become possible when everyone carries the burden."

She met his gaze. "I can't accept your terms because I've seen what happens when voices matter. When strength serves cooperation instead of crushing it."

"Then you choose war," Calypso said.

"No. You're choosing war. I'm choosing to defend what we've built. That's different."

An orange-striped figure strutted forward. Raizo. Taller, glossier, and unbearably pleased with himself.

"Perhaps a more elegant solution," he purred.

Calypso's tail flicked, but he didn't silence him.

"This entire quarrel is... limited thinking," Raizo continued, pacing like a lecturer savoring applause. "Strength versus cooperation? Order versus chaos? False binaries!"

"And you see the answer?" Nugget asked flatly.

"I see synthesis." He smiled with polished superiority. "Natural strength, guided by practical wisdom. Not brutality. Not naïve idealism. A third way."

Calypso growled: "Raizo—"

"Clearer minds see what others cannot." Raizo's tone suggested he was that mind. "An observer with a broader perspective—someone above the fray—can identify what neither of you perceives."

The implication was obvious.

Calypso's stare hardened. "And in practice?"

Raizo's smile flickered. "Well... naturally, the specifics require careful... deliberation—"

"Naturally," Calypso cut in, contempt razor-sharp. He turned back to Nugget, dismissing Raizo without a second glance.

"Your hour has passed," Calypso said. "Accept natural order or force me to impose it."

"I'll defend the choice we've made," Nugget answered.

191

"Then you've chosen your fate." His voice carried regret, not triumph. "I respect your conviction, even in defeat."

"And I respect your intent," Nugget replied. "But conviction doesn't make you right."

Calypso melted back into the trees. His army followed.

Raizo lingered, smile unbroken. "When this ends, remember—reasonable alternatives existed. Sometimes true leadership is stepping aside for superior judgment."

"I'll keep that in mind," Nugget said dryly.

As their enemies vanished into the dark, her defenders fell into practiced positions. The parley was over.

Finn nudged the ground with a paw. "Well, that was either very brave or very stupid."

"Why not both?" Kaya's eyes moved quickly over her notes.

Clive appeared, reports in paw. "Regrets?"

Nugget looked at the animals preparing to fight, not out of fear but choice. "None. We've built something worth defending."

In the distance, the approaching army announced itself like a storm.

Nugget touched her crooked crown. Tonight, it was no burden. Tonight, it was armor.

Morning would decide if it held.

The Night of Falling Stars

The attack came at dawn, exactly as promised.

Through the thinning dark, Calypso's forces moved with the quiet of hunters who believed the jungle already belonged to them. No ceremony, no noise — only shadows sliding across roots, claws flexing in the dew.

"Remember," Calypso told them, his tone heavy but uncertain, "this isn't slaughter. It's a demonstration. They see resistance break, they bow, and the order returns."

The words were firm. His eyes told another story. And Clive's network had ears everywhere.

"They're moving," Clive reported to Nugget's war council, spreading hand-drawn maps across the meeting log. His monocle glinted in the lamplight as he pointed to carefully marked positions. "Three strike teams. Calypso thinks he's being clever—hit the food stores, the water sources, and your command center simultaneously."

Kassandra's head tilted, her brilliant red feathers catching the flame. "My scouts confirmed unusual movement in the eastern quadrant. Large cats trying to move quietly." She almost smiled. "They're not very good at it."

Bruiser snorted from his position near the war council. "Jaguars think they're silent hunters. But when you've got boar hearing, you can detect a twig snap from half a mile away."

"How long do we have?" Nugget asked, her voice steady despite the gravity of the situation.

"Six hours, maybe less," Clive replied. "But the good news is, we've been preparing for this moment since we learned about Calypso's network. Remember when I first told you about external threats? You insisted we start planning defensive measures immediately."

Nugget nodded, remembering those long strategy sessions after discovering Clive's spy background. "The monkey engineers have been working on those contraptions for weeks. The sloth artillery team trained in secret. Even the coordination drills we've been running..."

"All leading to this moment," Kaya finished. "You've been preparing for war while still hoping for peace."

"But here's the thing about Calypso's plan," Clive continued. "He's still thinking like the old days. Separate forces, individual objectives, classic predator tactics. Each team thinks it's the crucial strike."

Nugget's eyes sharpened with understanding. "Which means he has no idea what he's really facing."

The Call to Arms

Before the technical preparations could begin, Nugget faced her greatest challenge: convincing prey animals to stand against apex predators.

The emergency gathering formed as sunset painted the jungle amber. Rabbits huddled in groups they'd seen in old territorial displays. Squirrels clutched supplies like they were preparing for the worst storm season ever.

"Won't lie," Nugget's gaze swept the clearing. "Calypso's pack is dangerous. Stronger, faster. Been hunting longer than most of us have been breathing."

A young rabbit's ears twitched. "Then why fight? Why not just... hide?"

"Because the golden feathers don't lie," called out a capuchin monkey from above. "The prophecy said this day would come."

Several animals nodded gravely.

A badger scratched his chin. "Destiny's hard to argue with."

"I saw them feathers glow," added an elderly opossum. "Don't glow for just anybody."

Nugget studied the small rabbit. "Because we built something here. Territory where rabbit warrens matter the same as jaguar dens."

"Plus," chirped a young finch, "better to be on the winning side when the prophecies start coming true."

Bruiser stepped forward, tusks catching fading light. "Used to think biggest tusks meant strongest voice. But the Chosen One here, she's got something different."

"The cowlick," whispered a squirrel reverently. "Just like the old stones said."

Kassandra's call came from above: "Sky-hunters used to rule airspace. Ground-dwellers stayed low, stayed quiet. Now we follow the Feathered Crown."

An elderly tortoise raised his ancient head slowly. "Seen seven different pack leaders come and go. But never seen one with the signs."

The capuchin engineer chattered excitedly: "Plus, our traps are blessed by destiny! And the sloths have been practicing their sacred contribution!"

"Here's what I'm asking," Nugget continued, though something in her eyes suggested she wasn't entirely comfortable with all the prophecy talk. "Not asking you to be brave cause you ain't scared. Asking you to fight because…"

"Because the stars have chosen!" finished a young wolf who'd recently joined their side.

"Because we're the good guys!" added a beaver.

"Because Nugget's got special powers!" squeaked a mouse.

Nugget's crest flattened slightly, but she nodded. "Whatever gets you through the fight."

Shoulders straightened. Chins lifted. The rabbits' ears stopped twitching. They were still prey animals facing apex predators, but they were no longer victims.

They were an army. At least in belief.

The Anti-Army Army

What happened that night broke every hunting pattern the jungle had ever seen.

Calypso's forces moved in their practiced formations; each group focused on its target. Nugget's defenders moved like water—no fixed shape, just flowing around obstacles and filling empty spaces.

Above, Kassandra's flyers ignored proper flight patterns, darting through moonlight in ways that would have made their ancestors screech in horror.

Messages spread across the canopy like gossip rather than formal warnings.

The jungle had become one massive trap, though calling it cooperation would have been generous. Weeks of work by creatures who built things until they worked had produced defenses that shouldn't have held together but did.

"Monkey crews, what's your status?" Nugget called softly.

A capuchin dropped from his watching post, landing with practiced quiet. "The blessed mechanisms are ready. And so is the divine launcher."

"Divine launcher?" Nugget tilted her head.

"Well, it's either divine or we got really lucky with the physics," the monkey admitted. "Either way, it is our secret weapon."

"Secret weapon?" Nugget tilted her head.

The grin widened. "You'll see. Let's just say the sloths have been busy."

Kaya raised a brow. "Sloths?"

The monkey crouched slightly. "Trust me. Give them enough planning time, and they're terrifying."

The Magnificent Mess

Calypso's assault began exactly when he'd said it would, which turned out to be its biggest weakness.

His forces represented everything dangerous about traditional pack hunting. Stratos led the eastern advance with veterans who knew every killing technique. Razor commanded sky-hunters whose formations had been perfected through generations of successful kills.

"This should be over quick," Raizo observed from his safe position. "If Calypso had listened to my suggestions about modernizing his approach instead of sticking to the same old textbook..."

"Sir, they're fighting back harder than expected," a messenger reported nervously.

"Fighting back?" Raizo looked genuinely confused. "Against proper military formations? Impossible."

But instead of finding scattered victims, Calypso's forces discovered something they'd never encountered: organized resistance that followed no hunting pattern they recognized.

When the first wave attacked, they found opponents who refused to follow the rules of how prey was supposed to behave.

"These ain't proper defense moves," one of Calypso's lieutenants snarled while dodging a perfectly timed counterattack. "They're making it up as they go."

"Exactly the problem," Raizo called from his observation post. "No discipline. No structure. Any competent force should cut through chaos easily."

Above, the sky filled with wings that ignored every flight rule. Kassandra's defenders abandoned formation flying for controlled chaos that turned Razor's coordinated assault into a mess of colliding hunters.

"Form hunting lines!" Razor screeched, trying to impose order on airspace that had apparently forgotten how proper aerial hunts worked.

Gray shapes darted up trees. Squirrels swarmed branches, cutting support lines and sending hawks tumbling. Below ground, tunnels collapsed and erupted, badgers bursting out behind jaguar flanks. Even the rabbits didn't scatter; they moved in tight groups, drawing attackers into dead zones.

Above, Kassandra's voice cut through the night: "Eastern advance slowed! Razor's hunters grounded! Western attack redirected!"

Calypso's ears flattened at the next sounds—his own forces roaring in confusion. Through the darkness came snarls and yelps as strike teams ran into... other strike teams.

"Your lieutenant thinks you called retreat," Clive's voice drifted from the shadows. "Your team leaders all got different signals."

Stratos roared in disbelief as his veteran hunters stumbled against opponents they'd never bothered to notice before. "This is madness! Prey don't fight back like this!"

"Problem with calling us prey," a rabbit shouted from a root bunker, "is we got tired of being hunted."

Far below, in tunnels older than memory, serpents watched through narrow vents. Silent, patient. The python matriarch flicked her tongue, tasting a battlefield unlike any she had ever known.

"Interessssting," she hissed to her fellow serpents. "The jungle changesss more than we anticipated."

Calypso rallied what remained of his forces for one desperate charge, muscles coiling for a straight path to Nugget's perch—when the jungle exploded. Not in panic, but in orchestrated chaos.

Coconuts rained down in perfect arcs, each strike forcing jaguars and boars to veer, stumble, and bunch together. The pattern wasn't random. It herded them like currents steering a trapped fish.

Then the vines came alive. Nets whipped down with whip-crack precision, yanking predators off their feet. Mechanisms hidden for weeks triggered in flawless sequence.

And then... the secret weapon revealed itself.

From the shadows of Sector Seven, a massive catapult groaned into position, wood straining under tension. The operators weren't monkeys. They weren't even fast.

"Sloths?" Calypso blinked in disbelief as the famously slow creatures moved with eerie, deliberate unity. No flailing, no wasted motion—just smooth, perfect timing.

Nugget's laugh rippled through the canopy, sharp with triumph. "Give sloths enough time to plan," she called, "and they'll out-engineer anyone."

The siege arm snapped. A gigantic net surged into the sky, spinning like a green comet. It hung there for a moment—too slow to seem threatening—before descending with terrible certainty. Calypso's world narrowed to the weaving shadow that blotted out the moon, then crashed over him and his remaining fighters like a closing fist. No one escaped.

Finn watched in amazement as the great jaguar leader found himself trapped by creatures he never considered worthy of notice. "I have to admit," he murmured to Kaya, "that's probably the most humiliating defeat in jungle history."

"And the most fitting," Kaya replied. "He's being beaten by exactly the kind of cooperation he claimed was weak."

Meanwhile, from his command position safely away from the fighting, Raizo watched the defeat unfold in horror, immediately looking for someone to blame.

"This is Calypso's failure," he proclaimed to anyone within earshot. "I warned him about underestimating the enemy's unconventional tactics. A truly visionary leader would have anticipated their desperate measures."

The Ideological Victory

Dawn bled slowly into the canopy, painting the battlefield in muted gold. Calypso lay bound beneath a lattice of living vines, his chest heaving, fur streaked with dew and defeat. The net didn't cut or choke; it held firm, built for strength but not cruelty.

Around him, the jungle moved with quiet purpose. Monkeys and boars hauled debris in rhythmic tandem. Birds wheeled overhead, their sharp cries punctuating a flow of orders as badgers directed the last of the tunnel collapses. Even the sloths—grim, unhurried—disassembled the massive catapult with the same precision they'd shown in firing it.

Nugget approached, feathers burnished by new light. "You fought like proper predators. Standard hunt patterns. Pack coordination."

She gestured at the mixed species working around them. "We fought like scavengers. Used what worked."

Calypso studied the scene, his analytical mind processing what he'd witnessed. "Your pack has no proper structure. No hunting order."

"No," Nugget agreed. "But we adapt faster."

For a long moment, Calypso said nothing. Then: "Traditional methods have served predators for generations. There's wisdom in proven approaches."

"And there's death in being predictable." Clive flicked his tail, leaning casually from nearby.

Stratos limped over, still bleeding from encounters his experience hadn't prepared him for. "Sir, they used irregular tactics. No proper hunting protocols."

"They used what worked," Calypso's tail lashed once, betraying his disapproval.

"Exactly," agreed another lieutenant. "Where's the honor in winning through tricks?"

Before anyone could respond, angry paw steps crashed through the underbrush as Raizo burst into the clearing.

He bared his teeth, tail thrashing. "This is outrageous! Calypso, your rigid tactics lost us this fight. A clever hunter adapts to its prey's moves."

The animals fell silent, studying the tiger who'd spent the battle advising from a safe distance.

"They won through deception and chaos," Raizo continued. "This wasn't strategy—it was lucky accidents masquerading as planning."

Calypso's expression hardened. "They won, Raizo. That's what matters."

"Same old hunt patterns," Raizo snarled. "Same old approach. I told you they'd expect that. We needed to be innovative."

"And where exactly were your innovations when the fighting started?" Stratos growled.

Raizo's whiskers twitched as he straightened. "I was providing strategic oversight. Someone needed to maintain the big-picture perspective."

The scarred leopard flicked his tail, voice low. "From behind a tree."

"The point is," Raizo pressed on, "Calypso's leadership failed here. What we need is visionary thinking that can match their... whatever that was."

He gestured dismissively at the mixed groups still working together around the clearing.

"What we need," Calypso said, "is to accept that we lost."

"Lost to destiny," whispered a young jaguar who'd switched sides mid-battle. "Can't fight the prophecies."

"Lost to superior engineering," the capuchin engineer said proudly. "Those sloths are geniuses."

"Lost because Nugget's got the touch," added a beaver. "Some animals just know how to lead."

Kaya tilted her head, watching the celebrating animals. "Lost because we stuck together. Right?"

Finn nodded enthusiastically. "Teamwork conquers everything!"

Several animals cheered agreement, though their reasons seemed to vary considerably.

Raizo looked around the clearing, seeking support, but found only indifference or outright dismissal. His followers had quietly slipped away during his speech.

"This ain't over," he said finally, then stalked into the jungle alone.

"Well," Finn said, "that was awkward."

"That was predictable," Clive corrected, making notes in his tiny journal. "Some animals never learn from defeat."

Nugget watched the tree line where Raizo had disappeared, then looked around at her celebrating defenders. Animals who'd fought for prophecy, for personal loyalty, for fear of being on the losing side, and yes, maybe some for cooperation.

"Got a feeling we haven't seen the last of him," she said.

"Course not." Calypso settled heavily onto his side. "Animals like that don't give up. They just get more convinced they're right."

The Battle of Falling Stars was over. The arguments about why they'd won were just beginning.

Taste of Victory

A flower petal drifted down and landed squarely on Nugget's beak as she tried to address the victory celebration planning committee.

"Sorry!" called down a capuchin monkey from the trees above. "We're testing the victory celebration flower drops!"

"Victory celebration flower drops?" Nugget blinked, brushing the petal away with one wing.

"Painted petals in coordinated colors," the monkey explained proudly. "Finn's idea. He said regular falling leaves weren't festive enough for commemorating our victory."

A nervous badger scurried up with a scroll made of bark, nearly tripping over a family of squirrels who were engaged in a heated debate about acorn arrangements.

"Your Majesty," the badger said, "the raccoons refuse to sit downwind of the skunks, the vegetarian animals want a meat-free zone, and now the birds are arguing about whether their aerial display should inspire hope or educate about flight physics."

From across the clearing, raised voices erupted as two monkey families disputed the proper height for banner placement. Meanwhile, a group of hedgehogs had apparently barricaded themselves behind a pile of decorative stones, claiming territorial sovereignty over their assigned seating area.

Nugget rubbed her temples with her wingtips. "Remind me again why we thought celebrating would be easier than fighting?"

"The problem," Kaya said, setting down her stack of organizational charts, "is that everyone wants their victory celebration to reflect their community's contribution."

She gestured to a growing pile of competing proposals. "The monkeys want aerial acrobatics. The boars want a mud wrestling tournament. The birds want synchronized flying demonstrations. The badgers want an engineering showcase featuring their tunnel systems."

"And the squirrels?" Nugget asked wearily.

"Want to bury time capsules containing nuts from the victory feast so future generations can commemorate this moment by digging up slightly stale acorns."

Finn bounded over, his usual enthusiasm undimmed by the logistics nightmare. "This is democracy in action! Everyone gets a voice! It's beautiful chaos!"

"It's just chaos," Kaya corrected, consulting her increasingly complex scheduling charts. "Beautiful chaos would be organized. This is eighteen different ideas of what celebration means, and they're all happening simultaneously."

A commotion erupted near the food preparation area where two families of raccoons were engaged in what appeared to be a heated debate over berry distribution protocols.

"See?" Nugget sighed, hopping down from her perch. "Even our victories create new problems to solve."

The berry dispute turned out to be more serious than it initially appeared. One raccoon family had meticulously collected and prepared berries according to traditional preservation methods passed down through generations. The other family had developed innovative fermentation techniques that produced berries with enhanced flavor profiles.

Both groups wanted their methods featured prominently in the victory feast, and both felt their approach represented the true spirit of the cooperative movement.

"Traditional methods honor our heritage," argued Stripe, the elder raccoon matriarch.

"Innovation shows we're moving forward," countered Patch, whose fermented berries did smell significantly more complex than the traditional ones.

A small crowd had gathered, and Nugget could see the familiar dynamic emerging—animals choosing sides, voices rising, the celebration spirit evaporating as positions hardened.

"This is exactly what Raizo or Calypso would have said proves cooperation doesn't work." The young wolf, who'd recently switched sides, kicked at the dirt. "We can't even agree on berry preparation."

Six months ago, Nugget would have panicked at this kind of emerging conflict. Not anymore.

"What if we're thinking about this wrong?" She lifted her head so all eyes could reach her. "What if this isn't about choosing between the old and the new?"

Both raccoon families looked skeptical.

"Patch, your fermentation techniques—how long do they take?"

"Three days for basic enhancement, a week for optimal complexity."

"And Stripe, your traditional preservation?"

"Immediate preparation, long-term storage capability."

Nugget nodded, beak pressed tight in concentration. "So, we have immediate-preparation traditional berries that can feed everyone today, and complex fermented berries that represent innovation and planning for special occasions."

She looked around at the gathered animals. "What if traditional methods and innovative techniques aren't competing—they're collaborating? Different tools for different needs?"

"A berry collaboration," Finn said. "Traditional foundations with innovative highlights. It's like a symphony where everyone plays different instruments but creates the same song."

The raccoon families looked at each other uncertainly.

"We could do a taste comparison," Stripe said slowly. "Educational and celebratory."

"And document both methods for the permanent record," Patch added. "Preserve the knowledge while encouraging experimentation."

The tension melted away as animals drifted back to their preparations, several pausing to ask the raccoons about fermentation timing.

They watched the raccoons huddle over their berry presentation. "That's becoming a pattern with you," Kaya said.

"What is?"

"Taking problems that feel like conflicts and reframing them as puzzles. Making cooperation feel natural instead of forced."

The Seeds of Delusion

Far from the celebration preparations, in a makeshift camp deep in the uninhabited territories, Raizo paced before a meager fire. His once-magnificent coat was matted and dull, his grandiose confidence reduced to bitter muttering.

"Look at that," Raizo spat, gesturing toward the distant glow of celebration fires. "Did you see how quickly Calypso folded? One defeat and he's bowing to a chicken, accepting 'honorable' losses. Where's his backbone?"

"Perhaps this is an opportunity for reflection," Vex suggested, landing on a nearby branch. "To consider what went wrong and how to—"

"Nothing went wrong!" Raizo snapped. "Calypso showed his weakness; that's what went wrong! A real leader fights to the end!"

Vex tilted her head, her sharp eyes scanning the celebration in the distance. "The jungle animals seem... content with their current leadership."

"Because they don't know any better," Raizo replied. "They've been fooled by simple solutions to complex problems. But you can't fool everyone forever."

Maw emerged from the shadows where he'd been hunting, his jaws still stained from his meal. "Maybe the chicken is just better at strategy than we were."

The words hit like physical blows. Raizo's tail lashed as he whirled to face the hyena.

"Better? BETTER?" His voice rose to a near-shriek. "I have vision! I have plans! I understand what the jungle needed!"

"And yet," Maw drawled, teeth flashing, "you're here with us, while she's there with them."

"Because Calypso betrayed the cause!" Raizo roared. "He just stood there while they used dirty tricks and false intelligence! Any real leader would have called out their cheating, demanded a fair fight. But no—he accepted defeat like some kind of honor code mattered more than victory! Because animals would rather follow comfortable lies than difficult truths!"

Maw watched this outburst with calculating eyes, then seemed to shift tactics. "You know," he said slowly, "maybe it's not that they disagreed with you. They just didn't dare to say it out loud."

Raizo's ears perked up slightly. "You think they knew I was right, but just... lacked the courage to admit it?"

"Absolutely," Maw grin spread wide. "Your vision was superior. Your understanding is deeper. Everyone knows it in their hearts."

"Yes!" Raizo's confidence began to rebuild like a fire catching new kindling. "They just weren't ready for my leadership yet. They needed time to understand the sophistication of my approach and see the flaws in theirs."

"Exactly," Vex added from above, her voice taking on a more respectful tone. "True visionaries are often misunderstood by their contemporaries. History will vindicate your methods."

"It's not my fault they couldn't appreciate strategic brilliance," Raizo continued, pacing with renewed energy. "If anything, their rejection proves how right I was. Only inferior minds choose simplicity over sophistication."

Maw caught Vex's eye, both wearing expressions of satisfaction. Each word of praise was making Raizo more certain of his own righteousness, more convinced that his humiliation was everyone else's failure.

"In fact," Raizo said, "their temporary success just proves what I always knew. Calypso would have been a disastrous leader. He was never the right guy for the job."

"Exactly," Maw agreed. "We need someone with your exceptional qualities to lead this jungle."

The compliments did their work. Raizo's shame hardened back into certainty—he hadn't failed, everyone else had. Neither Maw nor Vex seemed to notice that their praise was making him more delusional, not less. Or maybe, they did.

For Tonight, This Will Do

Back in the cooperative territories, sunset spilled molten gold across the treetops, and the celebration was already in full swing. Laughter tangled with drumbeats, the smoky scent of roasted roots drifted through the clearing, and strings of fireflies blinked like living lanterns overhead.

Near the center, raccoon families fussed proudly over tables lined with jars—berry preserves gleaming like rubies, alongside clay pots of something pungent and fizzy. Curious animals leaned close, sniffing, tasting, arguing about which batch packed the best kick. Beyond them, a pair of capuchins juggled while a troupe of frogs slapped rhythms on overturned gourds, their beats messy but infectious.

On her makeshift throne—a hollowed coconut propped on vines—Nugget watched it all, feathers puffed against the evening breeze. Pride swelled in her chest, light and delicate as the paper lanterns bobbing overhead. Still, it didn't quiet the tightness in her gut.

"Penny for your thoughts," Clive's voice drifted from beside her as he materialized from the shadows.

Nugget gave a dry cluck. "Thinking about tomorrow."

Clive tilted his head. "The systems you've built seem... durable. Shared power. Multiple safeguards."

"They're only as strong as the animals running them." Her gaze tracked a badger and a pangolin laughing over a spilled drink. "Animals change."

"Raizo," Clive guessed.

Nugget didn't answer, but her wings flexed.

"You fear corruption," he said.

"I fear comfort," she corrected. "Success makes you slow. Makes you think you've won for good."

Clive's voice softened, almost conspiratorial. "Also— for the record—this victory had less to do with cooperation than you might think."

Her beak tilted toward him. "What do you mean?"

"The false orders, the misdirection—that wasn't cooperation. That was... Traditional intelligence work."

Nugget frowned. "You're saying—"

"That your 'united forces' succeeded mainly because I sabotaged Calypso's communication systems." He adjusted his monocle, unbothered. "The sloths' catapult was charming, but the real victory came from old-fashioned spying."

Nugget's feathers prickled. "So, we won through the very methods we claim to oppose?"

"Plus," Clive said, "a heavy dose of luck. If Calypso had brought twice as many forces, or if Raizo had been competent, your cooperative ideals would be decorating someone's victory feast right now."

A passing monkey overheard just enough to misinterpret. "Modest as always, Your Majesty! But we all saw it—teamwork conquers tyranny!" He scampered off before either of them could reply.

Clive sighed, watching the fireflies scatter as dancers twirled through the clearing. "They need the story more than they need the truth."

The drums surged, wild and imperfect. For all its chaos, the moment felt honest in a way crowns and titles never had. Nugget pressed her worries down like an egg under straw.

"For tonight," she said finally, "this will do."

Then the jungle answered. A roar split the night—long, jagged, echoing like steel dragged across stone.

The music faltered, just for a heartbeat. Nugget froze. The sound crawled under her feathers, sank deep into her bones.

When the drums stumbled back to life, laughter rising to cover the silence, the chill remained. Some problems, she thought grimly, don't stay solved just because you solved them once.

Praise is Poison

The jungle was quiet that night—too quiet for Raizo's liking. No applause. No whispers of admiration. Just the croak of frogs and the restless hum of insects. He lay sprawled on a flat stone near the edge of camp, grooming his perfect stripes for the third time in an hour.

"They cheated." He jabbed a claw at the ground. "That's the only reason they won. Tricks and lies. Any fool can see it."

The frogs didn't answer. Neither did the trees.

He stared at his reflection in a shallow pool nearby. The face that looked back at him was magnificent— broad muzzle, flawless markings, amber eyes that spoke of dominance. He tilted his head slightly, admiring the symmetry. That face belonged on a throne. Not licking its wounds in the dirt.

"Lost because of cheating," he said again, louder this time, as if the night air needed convincing. "Not because they were better. They weren't better."

"Of course they weren't," came a smooth voice from the shadows.

Raizo's ears twitched. Vex dropped lightly from a branch above, her feathers glistening in the moonlight. Behind her slinked Maw, all sharp angles and sharper teeth. They moved with the confidence of predators who knew they belonged everywhere—and feared nothing.

"They couldn't outthink you, Raizo," Vex continued, her tone silk and honey. "Everyone saw how brilliant your plan was."

"Brilliant," Maw echoed, flashing a grin that might have been friendly. "If Calypso had listened, the battle would've been ours."

The words sent warmth spreading through Raizo's chest. He tried to keep his expression neutral, but found himself straightening with pride despite his efforts.

"Obviously." He stretched lazily, eyes narrowing. "But you can't reason with fools. They never recognize real talent."

"They will," Vex said softly, stepping closer. Her eyes gleamed like polished obsidian. "Once the right animal shows them what leadership looks like."

Raizo's pupils dilated with interest.

"You think they don't already know?" he asked, his voice casual but edged with hunger.

"Oh, some do," Vex purred. "The clever ones. The strong ones. Animals like us."

"And the rest?" Maw asked with a sharp chuckle. "The blind, the weak—they need help. Someone to… guide them."

Raizo turned toward the pool again, studying the reflection that now looked brighter, fiercer. Their words warmed him like sunlight on his fur. *They see it. They understand.*

"I suppose," he said slowly, "it wouldn't hurt if someone reminded the jungle what real strength looks like."

Vex's beak curved in approval. "Not someone, Raizo. You. Who else has your vision? Your courage?"

His chest swelled. Vision. Courage. Words that tasted sweet and dangerous on his tongue.

"I did warn Calypso," he said. "He was naive. And what happened? We lost to a chicken."

"Not because you were wrong," Maw said quickly, circling him like a shark savoring blood in the water. "Because he was. You had the right ideas. He didn't have the spine to act on them."

Raizo's whiskers twitched. The thought felt good. Right.

"He lacked… decisiveness," he said, his voice dropping to something darker.

"Exactly," Vex said. "Leadership isn't about fairness. It's about strength. The strong protect the weak—*but only if the weak know their place.*"

229

Something stirred in Raizo then, something dark and coiled. The words slid into his mind and stayed there, curling like smoke. *Only if they know their place.*

"What if they refuse?" he asked, though he already knew the answer he wanted.

"Then you teach them." Maw's grin widened. "And you're a very patient teacher, aren't you?"

Raizo's lips parted in a slow smile. For the first time since the Battle of Fallen Stars, the ache of humiliation dulled, replaced by something harder.

"Yes," he said softly. "I can teach them. I am a very good teacher."

The vulture and the hyena shared a look—quick, sharp, satisfied. The trap was closing, and Raizo was stepping into it gladly.

"We believe in you," Vex said, her voice a silken blade. "The jungle needs someone strong enough to lead. Someone who won't bow to barnyard nobodies."

Raizo's claws flexed against the stone. The pool before him rippled with the movement, distorting his reflection—but he didn't notice. He wasn't looking at who he was anymore. He was seeing who he could become.

"You're right." His tone deepened, smooth and commanding. "This jungle deserves better. *I* deserve better."

"Say it louder," Maw urged, his laughter low and hungry.

Raizo lifted his head, eyes blazing like embers in the dark.

"I deserve better!" he roared, the sound ripping through the stillness, scattering birds into the night sky.

The frogs fell silent. The jungle listened.

Behind him, Vex and Maw smiled like architects admiring their masterpiece. They had found the crack in his armor and poured their poison through. Praise, sweet and toxic, had done its work.

Raizo didn't notice the taste. He only knew it felt good.

And for the first time, he wasn't thinking about Calypso's failure. He was thinking about power—and how much sweeter it would feel than praise.

The Hollow Throne

Deep in the Thornback Territories, where the canopy clawed the last threads of daylight from the sky, Calypso stared at the maps etched into stone. Crude lines marked territories he no longer controlled. The Battle of Falling Stars had stripped him bare—his plans shattered, his authority fractured. For the first time in years, the jaguar doubted the one thing he had always believed in: the natural right of the strong to rule.

A burst of laughter snapped through the cavern like a whip. He didn't look up. He didn't have to. Raizo's voice carried easily over the murmur of the others.

"—and that's when I realized their entire system was a fraud," the tiger was saying. He puffed out his chest. "Fake orders, forged messages, all of it designed to make me look incompetent. Pathetic, really. But I saw through it—because I have the kind of mind no one else seems to appreciate."

Another round of laughter—too eager, too rehearsed. Calypso's jaw tightened. He told himself to ignore it. Let the tiger run his mouth. Empty noise. But when he glanced toward the corner of the war room, what he saw made his jaw tighten.

Raizo wasn't holding court like an insecure cub anymore. He was standing tall, head high, shoulders squared, and the way Stratos leaned toward him—the way Vex's wings twitched in approval—told Calypso everything. They weren't humoring him. They were listening.

Calypso's voice came out colder than he intended.

"Tell me, Raizo." His eyes stayed on the maps. "Why should any of us trust a tiger whose greatest skill is criticizing other predators after the fact?"

Raizo didn't flinch. Once, he would have laughed nervously, tried to smooth it over. Not tonight.

"Because I understand what none of you seem to," he said. "Strategy. Vision. I saw through their lies when no one else did."

Calypso finally raised his head, meeting Raizo's gaze directly. "And yet you were the first to fall for those lies."

A sharp intake of breath from Maw. For a heartbeat, silence stretched thin as a wire. Then Raizo smiled—a slow, cold curve that didn't reach his eyes.

"Even the sharpest mind can be caught when everyone around him is blind," he said softly. "But I learned. And I won't make the same mistake twice."

Stratos, the scarred veteran, stepped forward like a shadow, moving closer to the fire. His gravelly voice was low, measured.

"You raise good points, Raizo. Sharp points." His eyes cut briefly toward Calypso, then back. "Tell me—what's your assessment of Nugget's so-called 'cooperation?'"

Raizo's ears flicked at the name, and something dark flickered in his gaze.

"It's a house of cards," he said. "Built on the illusion that everyone's equal. But it only stands because no one's challenged it properly. That ends soon."

"And who will lead that challenge?" Vex asked. She preened her feathers with deliberate precision.

Raizo didn't hesitate. "I will."

The word landed heavy in the cavern. Calypso felt his claws unsheathe against stone before he could stop them.

"You?" he said. A quiet thread of disbelief ran through his voice.

"You think this is a game for barnyard nobodies?" Raizo's voice sharpened. "This entire jungle has lost its mind—letting a chicken dictate terms. You call that order? You call that strength?"

He began pacing now, tail lashing, his voice swelling with every step.

"Leadership isn't a game of feelings and handshakes. It's about strength. Clarity. Animals like me—animals born to lead—shouldn't be bowing to farmers' scraps!"

The words echoed against the walls, hot and brittle. And yet, under the anger, Calypso heard something else: the hollow ring of old doubts—Raizo still convincing himself. For now.

Maw's laughter broke the moment.

"Finally, someone speaking sense." The hyena flashed her teeth. "About time someone stood up to this farce."

"And what happens," Stratos asked, "to those who don't see things your way?" He leaned forward, firelight catching the scars on his muzzle.

Raizo turned, his stripes a ripple of shadow and light.

"Then they learn."

"Learn?" Calypso asked, but the question felt heavy in his own mouth.

"Some animals need guidance," Raizo said. He circled the fire like a predator sizing up prey. "But my patience has limits."

"And if guidance fails?" Vex prompted.

Raizo stopped pacing. When he spoke, his tone was calm, certain, chilling.

"Then stronger lessons become necessary."

The silence that followed pressed down like a storm. Calypso could feel it—power tilting, sliding out from under his paws. The tiger was no longer performing for approval. He believed this. He believed every word. And the others… they wanted him to.

"Perhaps," Calypso said, forcing steel into his voice, "you should tell us about your recruitment strategy."

Raizo smiled, slow and sharp.

"Excellent, let's do that. I'll offer every group what they deserve. Authority for the strong. Protection for the weak. In exchange for one simple thing—recognition."

Calypso shifted his weight uneasily. "Those promises contradict each other." The words came out smaller than his usual growl.

"Only if you don't understand hierarchy," Raizo replied. His tone was condescending now—toward him. Toward Calypso.

"Better animals protect weaker ones. In return, the weak acknowledge their betters. That's balance. That's order."

"And if they refuse?" Stratos asked.

Raizo's answer came without hesitation. "Then they've chosen chaos over reality. And I won't let chaos rule this jungle again."

Calypso said nothing. He couldn't. He watched as Raizo basked in the glow of approval—Maw grinning like a hyena possessed, Vex nodding with sleek satisfaction, Stratos murmuring promises of support. The tiger who had once stumbled over his own insecurity now stood like a king in waiting. And for the first time, Calypso understood: this wasn't just a threat to Nugget's rule. It was a threat to everything left of his own.

Later, as the war room emptied and Raizo's voice faded into the darkness—practicing speeches about "recognition" and "respect"—Calypso stayed by the stone maps, staring at lines that meant nothing anymore. His tail lay still against the floor. His claws remained out, but they had nothing to grip.

What had he created? He wanted order. Stability. A return to strength. Instead, he'd unleashed something far worse—a beast dressed in merit, drunk on praise, and blind to anything but its own reflection.

And the worst part wasn't Raizo's ambition. It was how easily the jungle might accept it.

The Art of Corruption

Raizo stalked the game trail, tail lashing dust into the air. Everywhere he looked, Nugget's rule stared back at him: monkeys hauling fruit for communal stores, deer marking shared grazing routes, even smug little signs Clive had carved—*Harmony Zone.*

The word alone made Raizo want to shred a tree.

The Battle of Fallen Stars should have ended the madness. Instead, they'd lost—*to a chicken.* Now the jungle was even more drunk on cooperation. Predators taking advice from porcupines. Panthers debating "equitable distribution." A nightmare with feathers.

He tried the usual tactics—swagger, intimidation—but animals only smiled politely and quoted Nugget's slogans back at him.

"Predators and prey are partners now, Raizo."

"The age of dominance is over, Raizo."

One squirrel even patted his paw and said, "Progress takes time." He nearly bit her tail off.

By the third rejection, his smile had calcified. Fine. If speeches worked for Nugget, he could make better ones. Not a single speech, though—something sharper. Tailored. Addictive. Give each group a glimpse of the world they secretly wanted, then watch them beg for more.

Movement in the undergrowth caught his ear—a cluster of boars grumbling in the mud about lost influence. Perfect. The first crack in Nugget's perfect little utopia.

Raizo squared his shoulders, smoothed his whiskers, and strode into the clearing like a general reclaiming his army.

Raizo had found something intoxicating in this game—the power to bend reality with nothing more than confidence. Consistency was optional. Applause was mandatory.

The Strong Deserve More

"My powerful friends," Raizo began, addressing a cluster of boars still fuming over Bruiser's betrayal, "you've been slighted for too long. Under me, boars reclaim their glory."

Tusk, Bruiser's bitter cousin, grunted. "Glory, how?"

"Prime wallows," Raizo purred. "Choice foraging grounds. And most importantly—authority over the smaller creatures strutting around like kings under the chicken rule."

Another boar squinted. "And the other predators?"

"They'll respect strength," Raizo purred. "Your strength. The jungle needs firm hooves, not clucking feathers."

The boars rumbled in agreement. Finally—someone who understood their worth.

Wisdom Shall Rise

By noon, Raizo stood in the cool gloom of the root caverns, his tone transformed from bold to reverent.

"Wise serpents!" He bowed his head slightly. "You've been the jungle's true power for ages—silent, watchful, maintaining balance while noisy beasts grab credit."

The python matriarch studied him with ancient patience. "And you offer what?"

"Recognition," Raizo replied. "No more hiding in holes while fools debate policy. Under my rule, your counsel guides every major decision."

A young cobra hissed skeptically. "Even territory?"

"Especially territory," Raizo said without hesitation. "Who better to draw borders than those who slip through every shadow?"

Tongues flicked in the dark. At last—a leader who spoke their language.

Sky Without Chains

By afternoon, Raizo was perched high on a branch, his earlier promises to ground-dwellers already forgotten.

"Lords of the sky," he cried to the hawks and eagles, "you've bowed to earth-crawlers for too long! The canopy should answer to its rightful rulers."

Razor, a scarred hawk, tilted his head. "And under you?"

"Aerial supremacy," Raizo said. "Flight paths, hunting rights, storm-watch privileges—all yours. The sky shall never again submit to dirt-dwellers."

"And boundaries?" an eagle pressed.

Raizo spread his paws theatrically. "The sky has no boundaries. Your dominion is as vast as your wings."

The raptors puffed their feathers. At last—someone who understood elevation.

Justice for the Forgotten

By dusk, Raizo faced a crowd of misfits: badgers displaced by land disputes, porcupines who felt overlooked, and a few lonely mongooses.

"Friends," Raizo began, voice heavy with sympathy, "you've been abandoned, haven't you? While the chicken dotes on her favorites, who speaks for you?"

A badger grumbled in agreement.

"Under me," Raizo promised, "everyone gets attention. Personal territory assignments. Custom resource plans. One-on-one consultations from experts who understand your needs."

A porcupine snorted. "Sounds expensive."

"Nothing is too expensive for justice," Raizo thundered. "I've devised revolutionary efficiency systems—triple the resources, half the work. More for everyone, forever."

The crowd erupted. It sounded impossible—which made it sound perfect.

The Contradiction Problem

As the day's recruitment efforts concluded, Stratos approached Raizo with carefully concealed concern.

"Raizo," he said, "your promises to the different groups are... incompatible. The boars can't have prime territory if the serpents are making all territorial decisions. The aerial predators can't have unlimited range if individual animals get personal territory assignments."

Raizo waved dismissively, his confidence now unshakeable. "Details, Stratos. Those are implementation details. Once I'm in power, I'll figure out how to make it all work. Great leaders find solutions that lesser minds can't imagine."

"And if the groups discover the contradictions?"

"They won't," Raizo straightened, gaze sweeping the room. "Each group only cares about its own promises. Besides, once they see the benefits of strong leadership, they'll be grateful for whatever I can provide."

Stratos looked up at Vex, who had been monitoring the recruiting efforts from above. The tiger's grandiosity was becoming pathologically delusional, but it was also becoming effective. Animals wanted to believe in simple solutions to complex problems.

"Your confidence is... inspiring," Stratos said, his ears flicking back.

"My confidence is justified," Raizo corrected without hesitation. "The jungle doesn't need timid cooperation. It needs a leader who promises greatness—and delivers transformation. Nugget thinks small. I think in revolutions."

The Divine Revelation

That evening, as Raizo basked in the glow of his own speeches, a revelation struck him with the subtlety of a falling tree. Destiny. That was the only explanation for how perfectly everything was coming together.

"Stratos!" he called, nearly tripping over his own tail in excitement. "The prophecy—I've cracked it wide open!"

Stratos padded over warily. "Which prophecy?"

"The ancient one! The one every creature whispers about." Raizo leapt onto a mossy log as if it were a throne, his eyes blazing. "'When might makes bitter right, one born of fluff shall rise.' It's been there all along, waiting for someone brilliant enough to see it."

He spread his paws, letting the late sun ignite the sheen of his coat. "Look at this fur, Stratos. Tell me that isn't the most magnificent fluff in the jungle. And bitter right? Nugget's joke of a government—

predators bowing to porcupines—what could be more bitter?"

Stratos blinked slowly. "Fluff... as in feathers?"

"Metaphorical fluff!" Raizo snapped, though his whiskers twitched indignantly. "The prophecy isn't about feathers; it's about destiny manifesting in texture."

He ran a paw over his chest, then froze dramatically when he found a single stubborn tuft sticking up like a crown. "And behold! The cowlicked sign of sovereignty!"

He turned, eyes gleaming with a zeal that was equal parts charisma and madness. "'A cowlicked queen of earth and sky.' Queen is symbolic—gender-neutral, representing ultimate authority. This," he jabbed at his tuft, "isn't an accident. It's fate!"

Vex glided down from the trees, his grin sharpened by opportunity. "The prophecy speaks of one who rises when might turns sour... and you were the first to see through Nugget's lies."

"Exactly!" Raizo's voice rang like a sermon. "Everything I've done, every promise I've made, it all makes sense now. I'm not contradicting myself—I'm transcending limitations. Mortals squabble over consistency. Prophets operate on higher logic."

Maw bobbed his massive head slowly, awe painting his features. "A true visionary wouldn't be shackled by common sense..."

Raizo's chest swelled. "Why do animals flock to me? Why do my ideas sound revolutionary? Because I am the one the prophecy foretold. The jungle doesn't just need me—it has *always* needed me."

Stratos exchanged a look with the others, the kind predators share when they've found the perfect tool. "When you put it that way... it explains everything."

"Of course it does," Raizo said, practically vibrating with conviction. "This is my moment. The jungle will kneel—not because I demand it, but because the stars have decreed it. And those who resist..." His voice dipped into a growl. "Well, prophecy has a way of... trimming the unnecessary."

From the shadows beyond the firelight, two pairs of eyes watched the performance. A mongoose and a ferret crouched behind a fallen log, taking careful notes.

"The chicken never actually claimed that prophecy applied to her, did she?" the ferret whispered.

"Never once," the mongoose confirmed, adjusting his tiny monocle. "The crowds decided she fulfilled it and crowned her accordingly. She just... went along with it and tried to do the job well."

"But this one is actively claiming prophetic authority before proving any competence," the ferret said, sketching Raizo mid-gesture with dry amusement.

The mongoose snapped his notebook shut. "Clive's going to love this. In all the wrong ways."

The Fluff Ascends

Night draped the jungle in velvet, pierced by the glow of fireflies and the flicker of torches lashed to branches. Shadows swayed like silent witnesses as Raizo took the stage—or rather, the boulder he'd claimed as a throne.

He stood tall, fur catching the torchlight in molten ripples, his silhouette crowned by the jagged stars

251

overhead. It was perfect. Destiny deserved good lighting.

"Citizens of the NEW jungle!" His voice cracked like thunder across the hush, drawing every gaze toward him as if pulled by gravity. "Tonight, the chains of chaos begin to break! Tomorrow, we reclaim our rightful place in the natural order!"

"Where?" a boar shouted.

"How?" hissed a snake.

"What about—" began an eagle.

"DETAILS!" Raizo bellowed, cutting through their doubt with sheer audacity. "You want details? Here's the only detail that matters—under my leadership, every problem becomes an opportunity, every challenge a victory, every animal EXACTLY what they were meant to be!"

The crowd roared. It didn't matter that the words were empty; Raizo's confidence filled the clearing like smoke, intoxicating and hard to breathe through.

"But how do we know—" started a badger, too stubborn for his own good.

"PROPHECY!" Raizo thundered, his voice rolling like a storm. The sudden solemnity froze the crowd. "You want proof? You want certainty? Then hear the words spoken since the dawn of time!"

He raised his head dramatically, as if listening to voices only he could hear. Then, in tones dripping with sanctity:

"When might makes bitter right, one born of fluff shall rise."

Gasps rippled through the audience.

"Look at this magnificent coat!" Raizo preened, twisting so the light glimmered across every silken strand. "Have you EVER seen fluff like this?"

Murmurs of agreement. Truly, he was spectacularly fluffy.

"A cowlicked queen of earth and sky!" He raked a paw through his mane until the rebellious tuft stood like a crown. "Behold—the prophetic sign! And 'queen,' obviously metaphorical for supreme ruler of ALL realms!"

Awe began to eclipse reason.

"I am the one foretold!" Raizo proclaimed, his eyes blazing with conviction—or madness; it was hard to tell where one ended, and the other began. "Destined to unify claw and beak with wit, not war! Those so-called contradictions in my promises? That's not confusion—that's higher-order thinking beyond your humble comprehension!"

Cheers crashed like surf. Even those who had been skeptical now whispered feverishly: *The prophecy... it fits. It all fits.*

"Tomorrow," Raizo roared, "we don't just transform the jungle—we fulfill the ancient design! And prophecy, my friends, CANNOT BE DENIED!"

The crowd erupted, stamping, shrieking, trumpeting, chanting his name like a hymn. Questions dissolved in the heat of destiny.

By the time animals trickled away, their minds fizzing with visions of glory, a boar frowned at a hawk.

"Wait—didn't he promise YOU unlimited territory?"

"And resource control," the badger said, side-eyeing a snake boasting about his forthcoming intelligence authority.

But doubts were fragile things in the shadow of prophecy. "He'll figure it out," they assured each other. "Great leaders always do."

In his command tent, Raizo basked in the afterglow of devotion, tail curled like a scepter.

"Tomorrow," he told his inner circle with holy finality, "we show the jungle what REAL leadership looks like."

He had no actual plan. None. But what were plans compared to destiny?

The First Strike

At dawn, the jungle expected a battle. Instead, it got chaos.

"CHARGE!" Raizo's roar split the morning air as boars thundered forward, tusks gleaming, hooves drumming against earth that wouldn't hold them.

The first boar hit Kaya's mud trap with a splash that sent brown water cascading through the trees. Another followed, then another, each impact accompanied by increasingly creative profanity.

"This is supposed to be easy." Tusk hauled himself from his third pit, mud dripping from his bristles as he glared at the innocent-looking ground ahead. "Raizo said they'd scatter like—"

THUD. A vine snare yanked his hind legs skyward.

"Ooh, that's trap number seven!" chittered an excited voice from above. The lead capuchin engineer peered down from his perch, taking notes on a bark tablet. "Excellent spring tension! Though I think we need better padding for the landing zone."

Behind the defensive lines, Nugget perched on her command post, one wing shading her eyes as she surveyed the chaos. "Well," she said to herself, "this is either brilliant tactical confusion or the world's most expensive mud wrestling tournament."

A serpent slithered past Clive's position, tongue flicking toward the command center. Clive pounced—too late. The cobra had already spotted his camouflaged observation nest, hissing indignantly as Clive wrestled it into submission.

"Comfortable accommodations," Clive panted, sweat beading on his brow. "Five-star hospitality, really."

Another snake triggered a leaf-pile trap, exposing a secondary patrol route. Then another knocked over a carefully positioned warning system.

"They're not trying to win," Nugget realized aloud. "They're just—"

"Flailing magnificently," Finn supplied, executing a perfect dodge as a hawk tumbled past his ear. "Though I have to admire the artistic chaos. Very avant-garde warfare."

Above them, the sky writhed with wings. Razor's hawks dove without formation, crashing into Kassandra's organized defenders like stones through spider webs. Feathers exploded in all directions as birds collided, tumbled, and shrieked.

"Form up!" Kassandra's voice cut through the aerial mayhem as she wheeled past a diving hawk. "Diamond formation, intercept pattern three!"

Her disciplined flyers tried to reorganize, but every tactical adjustment met fresh chaos.

"This is impossible!" Razor's voice cracked as he swerved around a sparrow half his size. The tiny bird darted between his talons with insulting ease.

Kassandra's tactical formations unraveled. Every time her defenders organized to counter one chaotic wave, another attacked from an impossible angle. Communication birds scattered like startled leaves, leaving ground units blind.

Below, wolves that should have been contained in the eastern sector suddenly appeared, charging through the supposedly secure western approach. Nugget's head swiveled, tracking the breakdown of her careful defensive lines.

"Bruiser!" she called. "Eastern breach!"

"I see it!" The massive boar thundered into position, his loyal followers flanking him. "These young wolves need to learn some manners!"

He charged to meet the escaped attackers, and the collision sounded like boulders crashing together.

"Nothing personal," Bruiser grunted, using his tusks to flip a wolf into a convenient mud pit. "But you picked the wrong side of this argument!"

"Kaya," Nugget called, "how are you holding—"

A snarl interrupted her. Kaya stood braced against two attacking wolves, her injured leg trembling under the strain. Blood seeped through her fur from a fresh shoulder wound, but her stance remained rock-solid.

"Still standing," Kaya growled through gritted teeth, parrying a claw swipe with surgical precision. "But this is like trying to organize a dance while someone keeps changing the music."

She pivoted, using her good leg to sweep one wolf into the other. Both tumbled into a conveniently placed thornbush.

"And the music," she added, breathing hard, "is apparently performed by a very drunk orchestra."

From the trees above, a slow, deliberate voice drifted down. "Patience... builds... strength."

One of the sloths was methodically adjusting something in the canopy—a massive contraption of vines and counterweights that had taken weeks to position.

"Almost... ready," the sloth continued with maddening calm as chaos raged below. "Precision... requires... time."

Nugget's claws tightened on her perch as she watched supply crates explode under boar hooves. Precious grain scattered across the mud—food meant to last through the dry season, now feeding the earth instead of her people.

"Counterattack?" Finn asked, muscles coiled for action.

"Not yet," came a measured voice from nearby. Another sloth hung motionless from a branch, observing the battle with ancient patience. "They... will... tire. Chaos... cannot... sustain... itself."

"No," Nugget's eyes narrowed in calculation. "They're not organized enough to counterattack effectively. But they're chaotic enough to turn any aggressive move into a disaster."

She studied the battlefield, her mind racing through possibilities. Every option led to greater losses.

"We hold," she decided. "Let them exhaust themselves against our defenses. Chaos burns out faster than coordination."

A boar crashed through another barricade, sending planks flying. Nuts scattered like confetti from a broken storage container.

"Look!" Tusk bellowed, finally free of his vine trap. "We broke through!"

Behind him, three more boars were thoroughly tangled in defensive snares, squealing in frustration.

"Ooh!" The capuchin engineer bounced excitedly. "Should we deploy the experimental equipment? The stuff we haven't tested yet?"

"Save it," Nugget called back. "We're not that desperate yet."

"Aw, but the untested stuff is the most fun!"

"Finn," Nugget called, "I need you to—"

"On it." Finn was already moving, bounding toward Kaya's position where fresh attackers approached. "Time for some impromptu choreography!"

He leaped into the fray with a flourish that somehow managed to look both ridiculous and effective, using a combination of acrobatics and sheer showmanship to confuse the attacking wolves.

"Ladies and gentlemen," Finn ducked under a swipe of claws with a grin. "Tonight's performance features 'Chaos Meets Calculated Response,' with special guest appearances by several very confused predators!"

One wolf stopped mid-charge, clearly baffled by the running commentary.

From above, Kassandra dove past in pursuit of a hawk, calling out tactical updates: "Message line compromised! Ground units, switch to visual signals!"

The sloth's voice drifted down again: "Now... would be... optimal... timing."

A massive net swept through the air with surprising speed, catching three attacking wolves in its weave and depositing them gently but firmly in a prepared holding area.

"Precision... timing." The sloth's slow smile spread across his face.

From her command post, Nugget coordinated the defense with grim efficiency. Injured animals to the medical stations. Reserves to plug the gaps. Communication runners to replace the scattered birds.

Every decision balanced preservation against response, careful calculation against the unpredictable mayhem Raizo had unleashed.

Despite the losses—the supplies, the exposed positions, the wounded—her forces held. Raizo's chaos was breaking against their organization like waves against stone.

But waves could erode even stone, given enough time.

The Ceasefire

By afternoon, both sides were battered. Raizo's forces were scattered, but they'd inflicted real damage.

Calypso appeared under a white flag.

"This has gone far enough," he said. "Animals are getting hurt, resources destroyed, and neither side can claim victory."

"No good reason?" Raizo sputtered. "Look at what we accomplished! We broke defenses! We destroyed their supply lines! We're clearly winning!"

"This is chaos, not victory," Calypso corrected.

"I demand complete surrender!" Raizo roared, gesturing to the smoking depot.

"You're both bleeding," Calypso said bluntly. "Continuing this serves no one."

Nugget nodded reluctantly. They needed time to treat the wounded and assess the damage.

The Spin Campaign

Raizo paced before his battered forces, mud still caked in his fur, tail lashing with renewed energy.

"Did you see that?" Raizo gestured wildly at the smoking supply depot. "We shattered their 'impregnable' defenses!"

Tusk shifted uncomfortably, picking thorns from his hide. "But boss, I got stuck in three different—"

"Diversions!" Raizo spun toward the boar, eyes blazing. "You think those mud-pits were accidents? Masterful misdirection while our main force struck where it mattered!"

He bounded onto a fallen log, striking a heroic pose. "Every trap you triggered revealed their positions. Every 'failure' exposed their weaknesses!"

Tusk's ears perked up. Another boar grunted approvingly. Then another. Soon, the whole group was nodding.

A young cobra slithered forward, scales still dusty from capture. "But Clive caught most of us before—"

"Intelligence mission accomplished!" Raizo's voice boomed across the clearing. "You mapped their entire surveillance network! Now we know exactly where every spy hides, every secret they think they're keeping!"

The serpent's hood flared slightly. "We... we did do that, didn't we?"

"Of course you did!" Raizo leaped down, circling the cobra with predatory grace. "Brilliant reconnaissance work. Couldn't have planned it better myself!"

Razor landed heavily on a branch, one wing trailing. "The aerial assault was a disaster. Birds crashing into each other, no formation, complete—"

"Brilliantly unpredictable!" Raizo cut him off. "You think military precision would have worked against Kassandra? She'd have countered every move! But chaos?" He laughed, the sound sharp and confident. "Chaos forced them to abandon their positions, scatter their communications, waste resources on damage control!"

Razor's beak opened, then closed. He cocked his head, measuring his response.

A young wolf limped closer, favoring his left paw. "What about the ceasefire? Doesn't that mean we—"

"Calypso's weakness." Raizo's voice turned cold, calculated. "He lacks the vision to see victory when it's within reach. Courage without commitment is just cowardice dressed up in honor codes."

He paced again, building momentum. "Real leaders finish what they start. They don't negotiate from positions of strength—they press their advantages until the enemy surrenders completely!"

The gathered animals stirred, murmurs rippling through the crowd.

"But we were pretty beaten up, too," Tusk ventured.

"Surface wounds!" Raizo dismissed with a wave. "Did you see them? Nugget could barely coordinate her forces. Kaya was bleeding from multiple injuries. Their supply lines are crippled, their communications destroyed, their morale shattered!"

His voice rose to a crescendo. "We were moments away from total victory when Calypso's outdated sense of 'honor' snatched defeat from the jaws of triumph!"

A cheer began in the back, spreading forward as animals caught the infectious confidence.

"Next time," Raizo roared, "we finish what we started! Complete victory! Total transformation!"

The crowd erupted, doubts dissolving in the heat of his certainty.

From the edge of the clearing, Calypso watched in grim silence as his authority crumbled with every word. Animals who had followed him for years now looked at him with questioning eyes, wondering if his caution was wisdom or weakness.

Is this what I wanted? The thought clawed at him as he watched Raizo preen before his adoring crowd. *A return to the old ways?*

But this wasn't the old ways. The old ways had structure, honor codes, responsibility to those under your protection. This was something else entirely—a carnival of ego disguised as leadership.

Calypso's claws dug into the earth beneath him. Yes, Nugget's cooperation was messy, inefficient, and sometimes paralyzed by indecision. Animals debating water rights while streams dried up. Councils forming to discuss forming councils. The weak thinking their voices mattered as much as those with the experience to lead.

But watching Raizo transform defeat into delusion, seeing his followers' desperate hunger for someone to tell them they were winning even as they bled... this was worse. This was strength without wisdom, power without purpose.

A young panther who'd served under Calypso for three seasons approached hesitantly. "Sir? Raizo makes some valid points about decisive action..."

The uncertainty in the panther's voice cut deeper than any claw. Calypso had built his leadership on certainty, on the confidence that came with natural authority. Now that certainty felt hollow, brittle as old bones.

The chicken's system has flaws, he thought, watching Nugget's distant territory where injured animals still received care regardless of which side they'd fought on. *But at least it doesn't require animals to believe lies about their own competence.*

Raizo caught his gaze across the clearing and smiled—the cold, satisfied smile of a predator who'd found the perfect prey. But in that smile, Calypso saw something that made his stomach turn: the absolute certainty of someone who had stopped questioning whether he might be wrong.

Perhaps the choice wasn't between perfect systems and flawed ones. Perhaps it was between systems that could learn from their mistakes and systems that couldn't admit they made any.

The Broken Promise

Three days. That's how long Raizo's patience lasted.

"They think I'm weak." He prowled the edge of his makeshift camp, tail lashing against tree trunks. "The ceasefire made me look indecisive. Soft. Like Calypso."

"Perhaps we should honor the agreement—"

"Diplomacy is for animals who can't win through strength!" He spun toward Stratos, eyes blazing. "I promised my supporters victory. Today, I deliver it."

Stratos opened his mouth, then shut it. There was no reasoning with that look.

In the medical clearing, Nugget fluffed her feathers as Kaya tried to rise from her moss bed.

"I should be coordinating perimeter defenses. And reviewing supply logistics. And updating contingency plans. Has anyone checked the backup water filtration system? Because if that fails during an attack—"

"No 'what ifs.'" Nugget held up a wing. "Doctor's orders."

"You're not qualified to be a doctor. Your medical training consists of 'eat berries and hope for the best.'"

"I'm qualified to tell my injured friend to rest. And as your Queen, I order you to stop planning contingencies for every possible—"

"CHARGE!"

Raizo's roar split the morning. Nugget's head snapped up as paws thundered closer.

"They're breaking the ceasefire!" Finn bounded toward them, his usual flair gone, replaced by raw protective fury.

"Of course they are." Clive materialized from five different hiding spots, each version adjusting a tiny monocle. "Desperation makes animals stupid."

The attack hit the medical clearing like a storm surge. Raizo burst through the line with his mixed pack, eyes fixed on Nugget.

"Surrender! Acknowledge my authority and end this cooperation experiment!"

"You broke your word." Nugget's voice cut deeper than anger. "You violated a ceasefire you agreed to."

"I adapted to changing circumstances. Real leaders don't let niceties prevent them from achieving objectives."

Kaya hauled herself upright, favoring her injured leg, and planted herself between Nugget and Raizo.

"You want her? You go through me first."

"Gladly." He launched himself forward.

Kaya dodged his first swipe. "Squeaks! Northwest tree, third branch, the thing I showed you!"

"The emergency coconut system?" A young squirrel's voice chittered from above.

"Deploy it. Now!"

Coconuts rained down in careful bursts, forcing Raizo's supporters to weave and stumble.

"You planned coconut artillery while bedridden?" Nugget asked.

"I planned EVERYTHING while bedridden!" Kaya kicked a lever. A net dropped from the trees, tangling two wolves. "Being stuck in one place gives you time to think."

From the canopy came a manic war cry. The capuchin engineers swung into view. "EMERGENCY PROTOCOLS ACTIVATED! Deploying all experimental equipment!"

Vine catapults snapped. Coconuts, mud pies, rotten fruit, and—

"Did they just launch Gerald?" a badger asked as an armadillo sailed overhead.

"Gerald volunteered! He said it looked fun!"

From his trajectory, Gerald looked like he agreed.

Hooves thundered as Bruiser crashed in with his team.

"Remember—we're not fighting because we like violence! We're fighting because we don't like treaty-breakers!"

"Is there a difference?" someone shouted.

"Absolutely! Intent matters. We're providing educational consequences for poor life choices."

Across the clearing, Clive seemed to be winning a private war against physics, appearing in multiple places at once.

"How are you doing that?" Finn called.

"Trade secrets! Also, family assistance."

Several mongooses slipped from hiding, each wearing tiny monocles. "Extended family. Professional development opportunity."

Finn turned combat into performance art, narrating as he fought.

"And now! For my next number: *Tiger Versus Unreasonable Expectations,* featuring interpretive combat and poor life choices!"

He bowed away from snapping jaws, then tackled his opponent with a flourish.

Then Calypso's roar cut through the chaos. "ENOUGH!"

Even the engineers paused. The jaguar stepped from the forest, amber eyes cold with disgust.

"This doesn't concern you," Raizo said, voice wavering. "I'm enforcing my legitimate claim to leadership."

"Your claim stopped being legitimate when you broke your word. Leaders honor agreements. Tyrants break them when convenient."

"You're just jealous that I succeeded where you failed!"

"You've succeeded at nothing except proving you're unfit for responsibility. You've broken treaties, endangered the injured, and attacked medical facilities."

The fight was swift and brutal. Raizo's claws raked Calypso's flanks but experience overwhelmed desperation. Minutes later, Raizo lay unconscious while his supporters stared.

"He's alive," Calypso panted, blood matting his fur. "Barely conscious—but alive."

"Why?" Kaya asked. "After everything he did, why spare him?"

"Because justice knows when to stop."

From the trees, the capuchin called down. "Should we launch the victory celebration coconuts?"

"Save them." Nugget sighed. "This doesn't feel like a celebration."

When Raizo woke an hour later, a tribunal faced him.

"You are hereby banished," Nugget said, sorrow edging her tone. "For breaking your word, attacking the injured, and violating agreements."

"Banished?" Raizo drew himself up. "By whose authority?"

"By every animal whose trust you violated."

"Trust." He rolled the word like it tasted bitter. "What gives you the right to speak for them? What gives you authority at all?"

The clearing shifted uneasily.

"Leadership based on prophecy? Golden feathers appearing when convenient?"

Murmurs rippled.

"If mystical validation grants authority," Raizo pressed, "then surely it can be questioned, reviewed, challenged?"

"You broke agreements," Calypso growled. "That demands consequences."

"Alleged agreements. Where was the vote? Where was the democratic process?"

A beaver raised a paw. "We did agree to the ceasefire…"

"You agreed. But did my coalition vote? Was there ratification?"

"Absurd," Kaya snapped, her voice sharp with disgust.

"If we believe in cooperation, shouldn't decisions—especially punishments—follow democratic rules?"

More murmurs.

"You call it breaking agreements; I call it tactical adaptation. You call it attacking medical facilities; I call it legitimate objectives."

"You attacked injured animals!" Finn snapped.

"Combatants in recovery. There's a difference."

Nugget's feathers ruffled. "The tribunal has reached its decision."

"Has it?" A cold smile spread across Raizo's muzzle. "Based on what legal framework? What appeals process?"

A badger spoke: "I motion to form a committee to review banishment procedures."

"Are we voting?" a squirrel asked.

Raizo's smile widened. "Exactly. I demand a formal appeal. Full democratic review."

Calypso stepped forward. "Enough games."

"Games? I'm requesting democracy—unless principles only apply when convenient?"

The crowd fractured into arguments.

"We could form a review board…"

"But who oversees the board?"

Nugget forced her voice steady. "The decision stands."

"Under what enforcement?" Raizo asked. "Who ensures compliance?"

Bruiser shifted. "We'll… make sure you leave."

"By force? Without due process? How authoritarian of you."

The animals shuffled.

Raizo smiled. "If I'm to be expelled, let it be through a legitimate process, not a decree."

"This is ridiculous," Kaya said through gritted teeth.

"This is exactly what bad-faith actors do," Clive noted grimly.

From the back, an elderly tortoise spoke. "In seventy years, I've seen strong leaders act decisively. Weak ones formed committees."

Heads turned.

"Perhaps some decisions require strength, not consensus."

More nods.

"We'll review the appeals process," Nugget said. "Until then, you're confined to the border zone."

"Confined by whom? Under what authority? What if I refuse?"

The questions lingered.

"We'll... work something out," Nugget said, though conviction faltered.

Raizo smiled genuinely at last. "Take your time. I'll be right here."

Stone and Stream

Three weeks later, a breathless otter scrambled to Nugget's perch.

"The river's changing course. Spring floods carved a channel through the Disputed Grove."

"How long?" Kaya unfurled her bark charts.

"Two weeks before the main channel shifts."

The grove erupted. Badgers demanded rights. Beavers cited dams. Squirrels wanted referendums.

"My family dug these channels." A badger clawed the soil.

"Our dams protect you all," a beaver slapped his tail.

"Everyone should debate!" a squirrel insisted.

"Debate water flowing downhill?"

From the edge, Raizo watched chaos with practiced interest. He had stayed in the border zone as promised—neither banished nor accepted, but always present.

"Friends!" His voice carried without strain. "Perhaps fresh perspective might help."

Some animals paused. Others deliberately turned away.

"The border tiger makes sense sometimes," a young badger murmured to her mother, who frowned but didn't disagree.

"He shouldn't be involved," Kaya said sharply.

"I'm simply offering observations," Raizo replied mildly. "My appeal remains under review. Surely speech isn't restricted?"

Murmurs of uncertainty rippled through the crowd.

Nugget watched this exchange with growing unease. Every reasonable word from Raizo chipped away at the clarity of his punishment. She hopped down.

"What if we're fighting over the wrong thing? Instead of who controls the bank, what if no one does? What if everyone shares it?"

"Impossible," a beaver said flatly.

"So, we manage it together. Build something none could manage alone."

The capuchin monkey engineers perked up immediately.

"Multi-level platforms! Water collection points for different communities! Swimming areas!"

"How?" a badger asked.

"Beaver engineering, badger digging, squirrel coordination," Finn said, warming to the idea. "Everyone contributes their strengths."

"Intriguing," Raizo said thoughtfully. "Though what happens during drought years? When there's not enough water for everyone's needs?"

Nugget felt the familiar tug of his reasonable questions undermining confidence. "We'll address those challenges when they arise."

"Ah, cross that bridge when we come to it." Raizo's tail twitched with what might have been amusement. "Though perhaps some contingency planning wouldn't hurt. Cooperation works beautifully until resources become scarce."

A beaver nodded reluctantly. "He's... not wrong about planning ahead."

"Since when do we take advice from exiles?" Kaya demanded.

"Since they make more sense than the chaos we're creating," the young badger replied, louder this time. Her mother shot her a warning look but said nothing.

Over the following days, the work began. Badgers excavated. Beavers engineered. Squirrels coordinated supply lines. Nugget found herself mediating disputes, solving problems, making decisions that affected dozens of families.

But she also noticed other things. How Raizo happened to be nearby when technical questions arose. How his suggestions, always framed as humble observations, consistently proved correct. How animals began seeking him out for advice, forgetting why they'd been told to avoid him.

"The foundation's settling unevenly," a beaver reported to the construction team. "We need to adjust the eastern supports."

"Raizo mentioned that might happen," another beaver said. "He suggested we check the soil composition there first."

"When did he mention that?" Nugget asked.

"Yesterday. He was watching the work and noticed the drainage patterns."

Of course he was watching. Of course he'd noticed. Of course he'd been right.

By the project's completion, they'd built something unprecedented—a riverside complex giving all communities equal access while improving everyone's water supply. Animals marveled at the engineering. The cooperation. The impossible made possible.

"Well," said an elderly tortoise, shaking his ancient head, "I never thought I'd see the day."

As the celebration continued, a young archaeologist badger emerged from the grove's ancient sections, clutching a weathered stone tablet.

"Your Majesty, we found something while digging foundations."

The tablet was covered in script that looked old but felt somehow fresh—carefully aged to appear important.

Clive examined the markings with his usual thoroughness. "Recent carving. Perhaps a few days old."

"What does it say?" Kaya asked, though her expression suggested she suspected complications.

The badger read aloud:

When feathered crown unites the stream,
And makes the impossible seem,
The first of trials finds its rest,
But greater storms shall test the test.

Gasps rippled through the crowd.

"The prophecy continues!" a finch chirped.

"Ancient wisdom revealed at the perfect moment!" added a beaver.

From his position at the crowd's edge, Raizo watched this performance with calculating interest.

"This carving is fresh!" Kaya said. "Someone made this recently."

"But it perfectly describes what just happened," protested a squirrel. "The timing proves its authenticity."

"The timing proves someone's been watching us and knows how to write vague poetry," Kaya replied.

"Divine inspiration works through earthly tools," the finch explained patiently.

"How convenient that prophecies always appear exactly when needed," Raizo observed mildly. "Almost as if they're created to explain events after they happen rather than predict them."

Several animals shifted uncomfortably. Others nodded as if this obvious insight was profound wisdom.

"Prophecy doesn't work on mortal timelines," a young monkey said seriously. "It reveals itself when we're spiritually ready."

"Ah." Raizo's tail twitched with amusement. "And how does one determine spiritual readiness? Is there perhaps a certification process?"

Nervous laughter rippled through the crowd.

Nugget watched the theological debate with growing frustration. "So we just proved we can solve impossible problems through teamwork, and your takeaway is that magic tablets predicted it?"

"Well," the young monkey said thoughtfully, "when you put it that way..."

But an elderly opossum thumped his tail against the ground. "Some things are bigger than explanation, young queen. Bigger than what we can understand."

Half the crowd nodded sagely. The other half looked skeptical.

"Should we vote on whether to believe it?" a beaver asked earnestly.

Clive tucked the tablet under his arm. "I'll file this under 'Convenient Discoveries' and let future historians sort it out."

As animals dispersed, Nugget noticed something troubling. Those who'd worked hardest on the project—who'd solved the engineering problems, coordinated the logistics, negotiated the compromises—were now crediting their success to mystical forces instead of their own capabilities.

"Maybe we were just instruments of destiny," she heard a beaver tell her cubs.

"The prophecy guided our paws," a badger explained to his confused mate.

Meanwhile, she watched more animals chatting casually with Raizo. Asking his opinion on unrelated matters. Laughing at his observations. The invisible barrier around the "exiled" tiger grew thinner with each interaction.

"We have a problem," she told Kaya and Finn during their evening strategy session.

"The project succeeded beyond all expectations," Finn protested.

"That's the problem. Every success makes Raizo look more reasonable. More necessary." Nugget's crest flattened. "Animals are forgetting why he was banished."

Kaya shuffled through her notes with unusual agitation. "Three families have asked me privately why we're 'still punishing him' when he's been so helpful."

"And yesterday, a group of young animals asked if they could invite him to their territory planning meetings," Finn added reluctantly.

Nugget felt something cold settle in her stomach. "He's not just waiting out his exile. He's using it. Every reasonable contribution builds his reputation while making us look petty for maintaining his punishment."

"Under my rule," Calypso said quietly from the shadows, "this conversation would have ended weeks ago."

Finn startled. "How long have you been there?"

"Long enough." Calypso stepped into their circle, his expression unreadable. "Exile. Enforcement. Simple."

"We're trying to be fair," Nugget said.

"Fairness is a luxury." His claws flexed against the bark. "One that manipulators exploit."

Kaya looked up from her charts. "So we abandon due process because it's inconvenient?"

"You must abandon due process when it's not serving you well." Calypso's voice carried the weight of hard-earned knowledge.

"But—" Nugget asked quietly.

Calypso's gaze shifted toward the border zone. "Reason is a convenient crutch to accept unreasonable leaders as excellent replacements."

The clearing fell silent except for distant celebration sounds.

"I should go," Calypso said finally. "Before I start making decisions that aren't mine to make. This kind of patience... It's not natural for me."

"Where are you going?"

"To watch him work. See what he promises the fence-sitters today." A wry smile tugged at the corner

of his mouth. "Your way takes longer. But it's...
educational."

As Calypso walked away, Finn looked puzzled. "Was
that a compliment or a criticism?"

"Both," Nugget said, adjusting her crown. "I think
that was both."

"He's right though, isn't he?" Finn said. "We're
losing ground every day."

Kaya shuffled her charts with unusual force. "The
data supports his assessment."

The three friends sat in uncomfortable silence,
watching a group of young animals playing near the
border zone. All of them laughing together. In the
distance, Clive remained unaffected, as if all of this
were simply another data point to catalog.

Across the clearing, Calypso watched Raizo in
conversation with a small group of animals. His
posture was relaxed, attentive. His suggestions met
with nods and appreciative murmurs.

Calypso flexed his claws against the soft earth.

The river kept carving new channels.

The End

www.ingramcontent.com/pod-product-compliance
Lightning Source LLC
Chambersburg PA
CBHW020239180626
46810CB00006B/2276